MURDER ON THE
BOWLING GREEN

MURDER ON THE BOWLING GREEN

Richard Derbyshire

Book Guild Publishing
Sussex, England

First published in Great Britain in 2012 by
The Book Guild Ltd
Pavilion View
19 New Road
Brighton, BN1 1UF

Typesetting in Baskerville by
Keyboard Services, Luton, Bedfordshire

Printed in Great Britain by
CPI Group (UK) Ltd, Croydon, CR0 4YY

A catalogue record for this book is available from
The British Library

ISBN 978 1 84624 712 5

Contents

1

Murder on the Bowling Green

Montague Darling awoke with an involuntary shudder as the town hall clock clanged and creaked its message of six o'clock in the morning. Until this moment he hadn't realised how resounding the bells could be at this unearthly hour. The reverberations projected a solemn premonition for the coming day. As his bleary eyes gradually focused, his befuddled brain slowly recognised the magnolia and rust shades of the wallpaper in the clubhouse. THE BOWLS CLUBHOUSE?? He almost screamed.

Slowly the cogs in the machinery of his mind spluttered into motion. A disturbing recollection of sleeping on a made up bed in the clubhouse instead of being tucked up alongside Mrs Darling in the warmth and comfort of the matrimonial bed filtered through to his brain.

A red mist descended in front of his eyes as the previous night's harrowing incidents flooded back like a repeating nightmare. A pair of ladies' evening shoes circled and tumbled around in his mind. Beautiful shoes in patent leather, high shine snakeskin effect with metallic slashes of bronze and gold. They had been thrust into his hands by Mrs Darling blustering about in various stages of undress. A sickly white cream covered most of her face, from which two menacing eyes peered out as if she were a tormented ghoul in cheaply produced horror movie.

'Montague darling,' beseeched his wife in short clipped

1

tones. As his surname was Darling, he never knew if the phrase she employed several times during the course of the day was a summons or a more romantic solicitation.

'These are the only shoes which complement the dress I am wearing for the dinner tonight.' She glanced fleetingly at her husband to ensure she had his attention. 'The tip of the sole on one of the shoes seems for some reason to have come adrift. I realise that it's only minuscule in appearance at the moment, but it could well deteriorate during the course of the evening. I have no intention of gliding around the dance floor executing the foxtrot with the sole of one shoe flapping in the air like a demented seal clapping for fish. Do be a darling, Darling, and do the necessary.'

She gave a small chuckle at her witty repartee.

Montague cringed. How many more times did he have to endure such infantile badinage? One would think that as they were well into their fortieth wedding anniversary year she would have got over the novelty by now.

'It's a bit short notice, my dear,' answered Montague in a low voice. 'I mean it's not as though they are the only pair you possess.'

'Don't even go there, Darling,' retorted Mrs Darling, her under lip quivering. 'They are, as I've already explained, the only shoes that match the dress. I do hope it's not too much to ask, a simple little repair job.'

From past experience of self preservation Montague knew exactly when not to force his side of the argument. 'I'll see if I can find some glue, dearest.' The face pack on Mrs Darling's countenance had by now hardened sufficiently to crack into fine splinters as she winced.

'You will be careful, darling?'

'Of course, my precious. Your every wish is my command.'

He collected his emergency tool box from the cupboard under the kitchen sink, knowing full well there was too

2

little time to venture out to the garden shed for a full complement of tools. Besides, the rain could be heard beating down in a steady rhythm on the conservatory roof. Unfortunately the only glue in the emergency tool box turned out to be a half used tube of superglue. He hesitated for a moment; he disliked the substance intensely. Ruefully he remembered the previous occasion he had employed the tube of doom. He had somehow managed to glue his thumb and forefinger to the toilet seat after attempting to mend a crack Mrs Darling had caused after consuming a five course meal celebrating the loss of two pounds on her latest diet. The indignity of passing through the crowded foyer of the Accident and Emergency department with a toilet seat glued to one hand was not one he wished to repeat.

As one would expect, the cap on the tube refused to budge. Having little time to waste he removed it swiftly with a pair of sharp scissors. Then, mindful of past mistakes, he carefully wiped the scissors with a damp dish cloth. With a free flowing abundance of clear glue he generously coated both the bottom of the shoe and the wayward sole. Perhaps he was a little too extravagant with the adhesive for it was obvious it would need some time to dry out to achieve the perfect union. He surprised himself with the brilliant idea of placing the shoe directly beneath the front leg of the sofa. Enough weight to keep the sole in place coupled with just the right amount of give in the carpet so as not to damage the delicate structure of the shoe.

He busied himself by vigorously polishing his own patent leather shoes and dreaming of the evening to come. The annual Bowls Club dinner and dance was always a splendid affair: a four course meal, the speeches, the presentations and then – his favourite part of the whole evening – the dancing. Soon he would be dancing his cares away. Although into his late sixties and a little on the chubby side, his nimble footwork always drew admiration from his dancing partners. A slow waltz, a foxtrot, and maybe even a quickstep or two. He disliked the modern form of dancing, standing on your own and flaying about like a demented puppet. He much preferred the excitement of being in close proximity to his dancing partners. Especially Nellie Prendergast, the Ladies' Club President who always pulled him close to her pendulous bosom. Then there would be Match Secretary, Vera Potts, who, although she had the annoying habit of sucking on her false teeth, always wriggled her taut buttocks in such a way as to administer to him soft murmurings in the trouser department.

Later, Mrs Darling presented herself in the lounge, almost the finished article except for two remaining curlers hanging down either side of her face. She looked quite fetching in a deep blue printed dress with kimono sleeves.

'Well?' she asked, taking in her husband's enquiring gaze.

'To my untrained eye,' Montague offered, not wanting to appear critical of his wife's endeavours, 'one side of that stunning dress appears to be longer than the other.'

'It's supposed to be, darling. It's what's known in the fashion as an asymmetric hem. I'm reliably informed this is all the style these days.' She leaned her head questioningly. 'Did you mend my shoe?'

'It should be nicely dried by now, my dearest.' Montague assured her. He carefully lifted the leg of the sofa to extract the shoe but found to his alarm that it refused to budge. 'Oh dear, it appears to be stuck to the carpet.' Gingerly he dropped to his hands and knees to appraise the situation.

'Stuck?' questioned Mrs Darling. 'If you've ruined my best pair of shoes, Darling!'

Montague inferred from the threatening tone that on this occasion the romantic version of 'darling' was not on offer. He pulled tentatively at the shoe, beads of sweat appearing on his forehead; a button popped off his shirt and rolled under the sofa. Mrs Darling exhibited signs of agitation but mellowed them with encouragement.

'Come on, Montague, give it some muscle. Anybody would think it was stuck with super glue.'

Montague made a rather sheepish gesture.

'You didn't? Please tell me you didn't use superglue, especially after the last episode?'

'It was all I had available,' he answered. Mustering his strength he renewed his effort. A blue vein appeared at the side of his head and began to throb.

'Pull, man, pull!' encouraged Mrs Darling, darting about from side to side as if refereeing a wrestling bout.

'I am dearest. I'm afraid that if I over do it I might strain something.' The result of his final effort caused him to break wind loudly, lose his grip and fall back on his haunches.

'Pathetic and disgusting!' scolded his wife, pushing him out of the way. 'You really are a nincompoop at times. Out of the way and let me have a go.'

She hitched up her dress and opened her not ungenerous legs in the style of a Japanese wrestler. Grabbing hold of the shoe she gave a couple of exploratory grunts.

'It's coming!' I can feel it!'

She stopped briefly to readjust her grip and to take in more oxygen. Montague quickly summed up the situation and grabbed his wife around the waist.

'Right. Together now,' he encouraged. 'After three. One ... Two ... Three.'

They pulled together in unison like members of a triumphant tug of war team. Unfortunately, it wasn't the shoe that yielded but a six-inch circle of best Axminster shagpile carpet attached to the shoe. The subsequent release of energy propelled the assailants backwards across the room until Montague's head collided with the writing bureau. This in turn caused the earthenware pot containing

5

Mrs Darling's much loved cherry-red geranium to topple over and deposit half its contents of John Innes potting compost and the plant itself over her newly washed and styled hair.

Recovering from the shock and cursing under her breath, Mrs Darling pulled the geranium out of her hair and set about thrashing her husband about the head until every last shoot had snapped off. Then with a final flourish she rammed the stalk down the inside of his crisp white shirt.

Storming her way out of the lounge she stopped only to pick up her shoe, still attached to the piece of carpet.

'Only you, Montague Darling, could come up with such a brainwave!'

She then threw the shoe at her husband just as he thought it safe to lower his guard. The heel caught him with a resounding smack on the bridge of his nose. The bells that were still ringing when the back of his head collided with the bureau yielded to fireworks exploding before his eyes.

The remainder of the evening's preparations passed in strained silence between husband and wife. Mrs Darling washed and restyled her hair as best she could and settled on a black strapless dress with full skirt, complemented by a pair of black suedette court shoes. Montague nursed the lump at the back of his head and stemmed the blood sufficiently from the cut on his nose to put on a replacement white shirt without risk of bloodstains.

Conversation at the Bowls Club dinner table was restricted to the bare minimum and Mrs Darling refused absolutely to step onto the dance floor with her husband all evening. This latter punishment backfired on her because during the course of the evening Montague enjoyed more than his fair share of dancing. Three waltzes pressed into the heaving bosom of Mrs Prendergast. Two foxtrots with the false teeth sucking, hip swivelling Mrs Potts. As an

unexpected bonus there were also several dances with the slightly inebriated Social Secretary, Maud Robinson. No shrinking violet our Maud, she presented herself at the Darlings' table dressed in a pink taffeta dress and gold dancing shoes. This was finished off with a bright red hairdo and a lime green flowered headpiece. Despite being overweight, perspiring freely and panting heavily she found herself well able to complement his intricate footsteps with amazing dexterity.

At the demise of the evening's festivities the weather outside turned most inclement, sheets of rain swirling about in the wind. Montague, in an act of appeasement, offered to walk across the car park and bring the car around to the front entrance. The tarmac was in a poor state of repair with several large potholes and just as Mrs Darling opened the rear passenger door to put her right leg in,

Montague's foot slipped on the accelerator. The car hurtled forward and Mrs Darling slipped backwards and was deposited unceremoniously in a large puddle of murky water.

Montague scratched nervously at the back of his head speculating on the course of action to take which could best defuse the delicate situation. The sudden appearance at the window of the mud splattered face of Mrs Darling solved the problem for him. Her wide-eyed maniacal countenance put the fear of God into him. With a wild shriek she flung open the door, grabbed him by the scruff of his neck and threw him face down into the same pool of oil-ringed water. For good measure she stepped heavily on his back before taking his place in the driving seat.

'If you value your life don't even think of coming home tonight!' were her parting words, loaded with appropriate blasphemy.

Now, staring up at the clubhouse ceiling and considering his predicament, he believed he had handled the situation with decorum. The despondent walk home from the hotel fortunately passed by the Bowls Club and he happened to be one of the chosen few who knew where the emergency key was hidden. He was off the dark unforgiving streets, had access to toilet and water facilities and could pass the early morning hours on a bed made up of an armchair and two padded benches.

Since the town hall clock had brought his troubled sleep to an end he reluctantly decided he might as well rise. Today was a new day, perhaps a new beginning. He switched the light on in the kitchen and caught a glimpse of his reflection in the mirror. The bruising and lacerations of the evening's follies were not improved by his mud spattered appearance. A quick wash and brush up in the men's toilet would soon repair most of the damage. On his way out of the kitchen something caught his eye, just the briefest of glimpses, which caused him to look out of the window and across the bowling green. In the early morning light he could easily have been deceived. He blinked several times in amazement and uncertainty.

A young female lay in a state of undress, apparently asleep, on the hallowed grass. He unlocked the door and leaned over the perimeter railings to get a closer look. Not only was she practically naked, she seemed to be wearing stiletto heels. The damage inflicted on the greens would be unthinkable. He cursed his luck. Didn't he have enough trouble on his plate already? Now he would have to deal with a young hussy who thought nothing of discarding most of her apparel and bedding down for the night on the bowling greens. He would soon teach her a thing or two about respect for other people's property.

Across the street from the municipal bowling greens old Sophie Brench closed the front door of her little two-up-two-down. With some difficulty she untangled the leash from between her matchstick-thin legs. Scotty jumped and yelped impatiently, keen to get about his business. Lighting her third cigarette of the morning she pulled the thin plastic mackintosh around her emaciated body. Eyebrows raised, she glanced up and down the street from behind thick glasses which magnified her eyes so that she took on the appearance of an alien. The dog propelled her across the street and into the park where he strained before her, happily sniffing from bush to bush. At a brief halt, and inhaling deeply on the cigarette lodged in the corner of her mouth, she glanced briefly between the leafy foliage of a large rhododendron bush. She observed the vague figure of a man running across the bowling green. Her blinking eyes followed him with curiosity. What she witnessed next she hardly dared believe.

Montague Darling in his impatient rush across the bowling green to apprehend the half naked, stiletto-heeled vandal

9

failed to notice a rather sticky patch of dog's droppings. Only when his foot stepped into the middle of it did he realise he had lost all control of his forward momentum. With arms and legs flailing like a demented windmill he tumbled clumsily to earth. He came to rest on top of the female form that held out her welcoming arms and outstretched legs.

The fall not only winded him but also the nubile young body underneath. She let forth a high pitched squeal from her ruby red lips, not unlike the breaking of wind. The force of the collision pushed her smiling face into his and her outstretched arms and legs simultaneously clamped him from behind in a passionate embrace. Two stiletto heeled shoes flew into the air. Together they rolled over several times, locked in this bizarre romantic union, finally finishing in the narrow ditch where, no doubt, countless numbers of over-weighted bowls finished their futile journeys.

Montague lay momentarily stunned at the bottom of the ditch with his paramour on top, her arms and legs still holding on in a position of fond embrace. Another ecstatic sigh escaped from her ever smiling lips. Only when he dared open his eyes and gaze into hers, hideously crossed and staring, did he realise he had become entrapped in the clutches of a full size plastic sex doll. In dire panic he struggled to escape. The last thing he needed was to be discovered cavorting on the club's hallowed greens in sexual collusion with a 'Loving Linda' or 'Willing Wendy', or whatever names they bestowed on these plastic monstrosities. The higher he lifted his head the more hers was propelled forward, her wide open mouth threatening to attach itself to his nose. After some frenzied exertion he freed his arms and pushed her away. As her body rebounded to embrace him again he aimed an upper cut which landed squarely on the smiling mouth. With arms apart her body recoiled from the force of the blow. For a moment she towered above him before toppling backwards, her wide open legs revealing a pair of black lace crotchless panties.

Hauling his bruised and battered body out of the ditch, Montague attempted vainly to brush the grass and mud off his grey flannels. He gazed bewilderedly at the plastic sex monster lying supine before him, her mouth now stupidly smirking and her legs wide apart, teasing him, inviting him. A feeling of utter disgust came over him as he perceived her owner could well have been engaged in revolting sexual shenanigans with this absurdity on these hallowed bowling greens. Greens which accommodated genteel Sunday afternoon mixed rinks, club matches and even the glamour and excitement of the occasional county game. His rising temper took control and he kicked the doll several times around the ribcage, hoping to deflate her, but she appeared to be made of sterner stuff. Refusing to be beaten by a mere doll, he picked her up, looked her fearlessly between the eyes and head-butted her. He recoiled hastily as his action caused something inside her to click and whine.

'Who loves ya, baby?' she squealed in a monotone voice.

11

Montague stared in disbelief. He administered a second vicious head-butt.

'Give it to me, big boy!' she pleaded.

Montague exploded with rage. He turned the doll around and gave her such a kick up the bottom that she cartwheeled halfway across the green before collapsing in a heap, her bottom stuck up in the air.

'Oooh baby,' she begged. 'One more time.'

In between thin blue wreaths of smoke that curled up from her cigarette and squinting through her thick glasses, old Sophie Brench witnessed these events in shocked disbelief. From behind heavy lilac blooms she had watched an agitated gentleman force himself on top of a half-naked young lady and the pair of them roll around in a passionate embrace. She had witnessed them kiss several times until, for some unfathomable reason, he had turned on his partner in great anger. Although her eyesight might be fading, her hearing was perfect. She had definitely heard loving pleadings ignored, and witnessed an impassioned show of affection repaid with a beating. What a shocking world we lived in! She gazed open-mouthed as the heartless brute now dragged his female companion behind the clubhouse. By taking a short cut through the children's play area she pushed through a gap in the fence just in time to observe the callous fiend lift the body of the now lifeless woman into one of the municipal waste bins. Sophie's startled eyes looked on in horror as the assailant endeavoured to cover up his evil deed by placing two large sacks of rubbish and some cardboard boxes on top of her. Sophie swore she would not allow this monster to get away with his evil crime. As soon as she returned to the safety of her house she would phone the police.

A short while later, Montague Darling witnessed two apparently separate incidents: the leisurely exit at one end of the park of the lumbering municipal dustcart after its early morning collection, and then, at the opposite, end the more hurried arrival with flashing lights and screeching brakes of the local constabulary. The slamming of car doors was followed immediately by an ultimatum.

'You! On the ground with your legs outstretched and your hands behind your head!' boomed a threatening voice from a megaphone.

An alarmed Montague looked around to see at whom these warning instructions were being directed. He saw no-one.

'I repeat! This is an armed response team! Do as you're told and nobody will get hurt!'

Montague glanced nervously, first at the police car and then all around him. He still couldn't fathom who they were after.

The voice behind the megaphone sounded annoyed. 'Don't keep shaking your head you idiot! Get down on the ground and do as you're told.'

Suddenly Montague realised they were actually addressing him. He cowered in absolute horror. An armed response team? What the hell was going on?

'This is your third and final warning! Down on the ground with your legs outstretched and your hands behind your head.' Detective Inspector Atkins knew that he loathed this suspected woman beater and murderer already. A defiant attitude of deliberately ignoring, or failing to show any respect for, the law always rubbed him up the wrong way. 'It's just as well we are not armed. I would have shot the stupid fool by now.'

Montague was of the opinion that some gigantic mistake had been made, but to be on the safe side he dropped to the ground as quickly as possible. He found it extremely uncomfortable lying face down with his hands behind his head. He listened as two sets of heavy footsteps approached. A spiteful knee thudded down in the middle of his back and a set of handcuffs were expertly wrapped around his wrists.

'Got him, guv,' proclaimed the detective constable.

'Good. Name?'

Montague felt a kick in the ribs. 'I said name?'

'Please don't do that. Darling.'

'Don't you "darling" me, you sex maniac!' warned D.I. Atkins. People like you make me sick. I'll ask you again. What's your name?'

'Darling,' repeated Montague in an almost inaudible voice.

'There, he's said it again,' fumed the inspector. 'The pervert keeps calling me darling.' He lifted his boot ready to administer further prompting. D.C. Carter stopped him in the nick of time.

'Guv, I think that could be his real name.' He waved Montague's wallet up and down.

'What do you mean?'

'According to this, his name is Darling: Montague Arthur Darling.'

'Well, why didn't the fool say so?' The two officers hauled the suspect to his feet. The inspector did as he was supposed to and inspected the wallet. 'Mmm ... Very interesting. M.A.D. for short. Well, Montague Arthur Darling, I'm arresting you for R.A.M. for short.'

'What's that?' quivered Montague.

'Rape, Abduction and Murder.'

They quickly read him his rights.

Montague looked about in abject misery. He recalled last evening as having been a bit of a nightmare. Furthermore, this morning hadn't started off too well, what with the sex doll and everything, but this latest incident was positively surreal.

'Yes, take a good look around you, Montague. This could well be the last time you see broad daylight as a free man,'

14

barked the inspector, opening the police car door and pushing him onto the back seat.

Montague struggled to sit upright; he hadn't realised until now how helpless you were without the use of your arms.

'There's been a terrible mistake,' he pleaded. 'I haven't done anything.'

'Funny! You all say the same thing, you pervert. Each and every one I've nicked and put away for a nice long stretch have uttered them very words,' smirked the Inspector.

'I'm innocent, I tell you, I'm innocent,' answered Montague in a low voice. 'My wife will never believe this when I tell her. She'll kill me.'

D.I. Atkins raised his eyebrows. 'Under the wife's thumb are you? Dominates you does she? Nag, nag, nag. Makes your life a misery? I've seen it all before. So to take your revenge, show your masculinity like, you take it out on some poor defenceless girl?'

Montague slumped back in his seat. He studied the back of the inspector's head and noticed he had a large brown mole right on the collar line. 'What on earth are you talking about? I'm innocent I keep telling you.'

'And if you're so innocent why are you sneaking around a deserted park at half past six in the morning?' asked detective constable Carter, unwrapping a mint and flicking the paper in Montague's face.

'I've just come out of the clubhouse.'

Both detectives burst out laughing. 'Oh I see, we're with you now. You've got hundreds of bowlers queuing up to get on the greens at the crack of dawn?' said the constable. 'Pull the other one, it's got bells on.'

Montague realised his explanation held little water. 'What did you say I'm being charged with again?'

D.C. Carter reverted to his notebook. 'Rape, abduction and murder. They'll probably throw away the key.'

'Of whom, though?'

15

'Of an innocent young woman!' shouted the inspector. 'Forgotten it so soon have you?' He turned to his partner. 'They're so callous, this type of criminal, it's unbelievable. They commit a heinous crime and then dismiss it from their minds without a flicker of remorse.'

'The psychologists say it's the only way they can live with it, guv,' offered D.C. Carter.

'What young woman?' cried Montague 'I haven't clapped eyes on a living soul since I left the clubhouse.'

'Unbelievable. Don't think you're getting away with all that loss of memory rubbish. The young woman you raped, beat, and then tried to dispose of!' glared D.I. Atkins.

'You must be out of your tiny minds,' retorted Montague, then instantly regretted it.

The inspector turned around in his seat again, his nostrils flaring. 'And if you're so innocent what are you doing prowling round in a deserted park this time of the morning. How do you explain the fact that your clothes are splattered in mud and your face is covered in cuts and bruises? Young lady put up a bit of a fight did she?'

Montague cringed back into his seat. 'I slipped on some dog's doody and Mrs Darling hit me with a bunch of geraniums.'

The detectives laughed in unison. 'Dog's doody and geraniums, eh? He's as nutty as a fruitcake this one, guv,' said D.C. Carter, trying to keep his hands steady as he jotted down notes.

The inspector took a keener interest in Montague's injuries. 'Must have been a big geranium to give you a bruise that size. Surely you don't expect us to believe that rubbish?'

'I got the bruises when she hit me with one of her shoes.'

'Ah! Got you!' A light of triumph gleamed in the inspector's eyes. 'You admit it then. You attacked the young lady and she tried to fight you off with one of her shoes. You might as well come clean, Montague. Get it off your chest. You'll feel a whole lot better.'

'No, you fool, the wife. Mrs Darling threw one of her shoes at me.'

'Don't you call me a fool, you're in enough trouble already. Anyway, why would your wife want to throw a shoe at you?'

'Because I glued it to a six inch piece of shag pile carpet. We were going dancing, you see.' Montague's voice trailed off hopelessly. 'No, I don't suppose you do see...'

The front seats squeaked as the detectives rocked helplessly back and forth.

'I told you, guv – nutty as a fruit cake.'

'Yes, this is one of the best yet. Remind me what we've got so far.'

D.C. Carter licked the end of his pencil and consulted his notes. 'He got up at the crack of dawn to open up the bowls club. He slipped on some dog's doody and his wife beat him with a geranium. Then she threw a shoe at him attached to a six inch piece of shag pile carpet because they were going dancing.'

'He's a lunatic, a raving lunatic,' diagnosed the inspector. He let out a long troubled sigh. 'Oh no, you're not going down that path, are you, Montague? You're not going to plead insanity? I hate it when people plead insanity. There's no fun in that at all. I tend to get very angry when people plead insanity. And when I get angry I...' He raised a clenched fist. D.C. Carter put up a hand to stop him.

'You don't want to make the inspector angry now, do you, Montague? I don't think that would be a very good idea.'

'I'm not a lunatic, and I'm certainly not pleading insanity,' protested Montague.

'Good. I'm glad to hear it.' The inspector breathed a sigh of relief. 'Have you got that down in writing, constable?'

17

'Yes, guv.'

'Right now, Montague, shall we start at the beginning again? You are being charged with the rape, abduction, and murder of an as yet unidentified woman.'

'Who says so?' asked Montague, still trying to come to terms with the unreality of it all. 'Where and when was all this supposed to have taken place?'

'It's no use trying to deny it, man. We have a very reliable witness who no more than half an hour ago saw you rape and viciously beat up your victim, then attempt to dispose of the body in one of the municipal dustbins.'

Montague began shaking uncontrollably. From his open mouth issued an eerie scream pitched somewhere between hysterical laughter and crying.

'I think he's cracking up, guv,' said D.C. Carter.

'I do believe he is. With a bit of luck we can have this whole sorry case wrapped up fairly quickly.'

'It was a doll! A flaming doll!' laughed Montague, his convulsions gradually receding.

'What's a flaming doll got to do with it?' asked a concerned inspector. 'And why would anyone want to set a doll on fire?'

'No, no, no!' pleaded Montague. 'What your witness must have seen was me and a blow-up plastic doll. It wasn't a real person. It was one of those life-size sex toys.'

'You want us to believe you were having sexual relations in the middle of a bowling green with an inflatable sex doll?'

''No!' pleaded Montague. 'I wasn't having sexual relations with anyone or anything. How many more times do I have to tell you? I slipped on some dog's doody and happened to fall on top of this plastic doll.'

The frustration caused by the accused's repeated contradictions had the effect of turning the inspector's face from pink to perspiring crimson. 'Our witness tells a very different story. She says she observed the pair of you locked in a passionate embrace and that you were both so consumed with sexual desire you rolled into the ditch.'

'I'm telling you it was a plastic doll!'

'The witness claimed she heard the woman talking to you. She couldn't hear exactly what she said, but she definitely heard a woman's voice. Plastic dolls don't talk.'

'This one did,' contradicted Montague.

'And what exactly did she say?' encouraged the inspector. Montague looked sheepishly from one detective to the other. 'Well, come on, Montague, what did she say?'

'She said ... "Give it to me big boy".'

The two detectives finally lost all pretence of professionalism and broke down into fits of laughter. They were only brought back to their senses when another police car pulled up alongside. D.I. Atkins lowered his window. 'What did you find?'

'Nothing, guv. The bin was empty.'

'It can't be! He was seen trying to dispose of the body less than half an hour ago.'

Montague thought he would cheer the inspector up – make his day, so to speak. 'The council made an early morning collection. The truck left the park just before you came in.'

'You crafty swine!' screamed the inspector. 'You knew all along. You had it timed to perfection.' He shouted to the occupants of the second police car. 'What are you waiting for? Get after that disposal truck before it reaches the waste site!'

The car quickly screeched away, then just as quickly screeched back again. 'What exactly are we looking for, guv?'

'You're looking for the body of a young woman, or a life-size talking sex doll.'

'A life-size talking sex doll, guv?'

19

'Yes, and if the pair of you don't get a move on and reach the tip before the truck you'll be spending your weekend sorting through tons of shite and heaven knows what else!'

The police car sped away again, the smell of burning rubber irritating Montague's bruised and battered nose. He fidgeted about on the back seat trying to find a comfortable position. 'Can you take the handcuffs off now? My wrists are starting to swell up.'

'No, we can't, and if you don't stop whingeing they won't be the only things that swell up,' said D.C. Carter.

'But you're not still going to charge me are you?'

'Of course we are!' shouted the inspector. 'I just don't know if it will be rape, abduction and murder, sexual deviation in a public place, or wasting police time and resources.'

Montague slumped uncomfortably back in his seat. He wondered which of the charges would lower him the most in Mrs Darling's estimation.

'What now, guv?' asked D.C. Carter.

'I think you'd better get over to that old dear and take a proper statement. She sounded a bit incoherent over the phone, what with her coughing and spluttering. I should stand well back if I were you – sounded as if she was about to cough her lungs up at any moment. I'll take Mr Montague flipping Darling with me and follow the other car down to the tip. I just hope we make it in time.'

On the journey Montague slumped down as low as possible in the back seat. He didn't want to be recognised on his road to shame. He wished they would throw a blanket over his head, as they did on television.

On reaching the tip the car halted behind the other police car outside the manager's office. Montague rolled forward banging his nose on the front seat and finishing up in the seat well. The site manager looked enquiringly up from his desk, annoyed that his tea break had been interrupted. He continued dipping his ginger biscuit into his tea. The biscuit had reached halfway from cup to mouth when the inspector entered pushing Montague in front of him.

'Not another one?' observed the manager dryly. 'We've already had two of your lot looking for something. They declined to tell me what they were looking for, so I couldn't help them, could I? Got a regular little crime wave going on, have we? Who's this?' He waved a ginger biscuit in Montague's direction.

'He's helping us with our enquiries.'

'Don't look your average type of villain. Looks a bit sorry for himself, if you ask me. Here, you haven't been beating him up, have you?'

'No we haven't,' replied the inspector, making a mental note that he didn't like the look of this person either. Too glib, too slimy. Might be worth checking him out on the computer later. 'Now the truck from Prince's Park. Has it been unloaded yet?'

The site manager took his time volunteering the information. He dunked another biscuit, licked his fingers and wiped his lips with the back of his hand.

'About twenty minutes ago. She's unloading now. Funny thing that – it's not your lucky day. She should have unloaded last night, but came back too late. That's why we sent her out early this morning like, just to fill her up. Anything from the park would have been at the back of the truck. It'll come off first see? So if your boys weren't quick enough, whatever it is you're looking for will be under about a ton of crap.

'Thanks a bunch,' said the Inspector.

'Don't mention it. Always glad to help the boys in blue,' smirked the manager wiping his tongue over black and yellow teeth. A constable from the second patrol car burst into the office dusting down his uniform.

'Any luck?' asked the inspector.

'No, guv, not yet. I'm afraid we got here too late. The operator said they had already shovelled one lot of rubbish onto the main pile.'

The inspector rushed to the window. 'You don't mean that ruddy great pile there, surely?'

'Told you it wasn't your lucky day,' grinned the manager. D.I. Atkins turned away from the window and switched his attention to Montague.

'It's going to take a month of Sundays to search through that lot. If I find out you're lying, Darling, you'll be for the high jump.'

A worried Montague averted his face from the penetrating gaze of his accuser. The moment the inspector moved away from the window Montague's eyes widened. He rubbed them in disbelief.

'There she is! There she is!'

'What are you blabbering about now, Darling?'

'The doll! Look out of the window!'

The inspector turned around just in time to see a gaping, ruby-red mouth and a leering, cross-eyed face go bobbing past the window. The constable reacted first, opened the door and invited the doll and her latest suitor to step inside the office. From under a hard hat that appeared to be several sizes too big for him a middle-aged workman in council overalls trying desperately to hide the doll behind him, looked sheepishly around the gathering. As he met the manager's inquisitive gaze his eyes dropped miserably to the floor.

'This is Bob Tucker, yard operative. I think the police might want a word with you.' The manager shook his head and dunked the last of his ginger biscuits before throwing the empty packet into the bin.

The inspector's eyes moved first to Bob Tucker, then to the half-hidden doll, then back to Bob Tucker. It was

22

obviously a close run thing which he detested more. 'Where did you find that monstrosity?'

Tucker in turn looked at the inspector and then at the doll. He attempted to straighten her hairpiece which had come adrift in her travels. He brushed some of the mud off the end of her nose with his sleeve. 'She came in on truck number three.'

'And what exactly were you intending to do with her?'

Tucker shrugged his shoulders and gave a feeble smile. 'I was going to take her home, clean her up a bit. Well, none of the other lads wanted her. Said I could keep her.'

The site manager finished running his tongue around his teeth. 'You know very well, Tucker, you're not allowed to take anything from this site home with you. Once it comes into the yard it's council property.'

'Yes, but the lads said we couldn't make anything on the side for the kitty out of her, so that's why they let me have her...'

'All right, Tucker,' intervened the manager hurriedly.

D.I. Atkins turned his attention back to Montague. 'Is this the doll you were having sexual relationships with on the bowling green?'

'I wasn't having sexual relationships with her. How many more times do I have to tell you? I was just trying to get rid of her.'

'That's for me to decide. Now, is it the self-same doll?'

'I'm not sure,' replied Montague, looking the doll up and down as if she were on an identity parade.

'What do you mean, you're not sure?' shouted the inspector. 'How many other sex dolls have you been having hanky-panky with today?'

'Well, I don't recognise her without her clothes on. The one on the bowling green had a sort of see-through vest and a pair of...'

'Yes?' enquired the Inspector.

23

'Black lace crotchless knickers,' mumbled Montague. All eyes turned back to the hapless Bob Tucker.

'What have you done with them, Bob?' asked the site manager. Without letting go of the doll, Tucker pulled a flimsy chemise out of one pocket and the black lace knickers out of another.

'I've a good mind to nick you for withholding evidence from the police, you little pervert,' said the inspector, grabbing at the clothes and then at the doll. But Tucker held on for dear life.

'She's mine. I found her first!'

'Give it here,' commanded the inspector. 'I need it for police evidence.'

'She's mine,' insisted Tucker.

'Actually, she's technically still council property, while she's on site,' the manager pointed out.

'Don't you start or I'll have you for obstructing the police.' The inspector returned to the struggle for possession of the doll. Being pulled violently from both sides she looked ready to burst. Her breasts became so taut that both her nipples flew off. She lounged back and then whiplashed forward banging her head on the desk. Both her arms were hurriedly released as a loud whirring began. She bucked back and forth as if in some convulsive fit.

'Me love you long time, baby, me love you long time.'

The inspector sank into an empty chair. He had put up with as much as he could take. His mind boggled at the thought of how much ridicule the press and his colleagues would throw at him if this absurd affair went any further. He gave first grace to Bob Tucker.

'Take your girlfriend and do what you like with her, as long as the pair of you keep out of my sight.'

Tucker's face brightened up. He collected his bosom pal, scratched about on the floor for her nipples and almost ran out of the room.

Montague looked relieved. 'I told you the doll talked.'

'Shut it, Darling. You should consider yourself an extremely lucky man, wasting valuable police time.' He turned to the constable. 'Take him out of my sight. Return him home or to whatever nasty little nook or cranny he crawled out of. Better still, take him right up to his front door and let his wife know he's been helping police with their enquiries. Let him try explaining his way out of that to Mrs Darling.'

2

No Fool Like an Old Fool

Leslie Stonewall Jackson awoke in a bedroom which, if the curtains had been drawn, would have been bathed in brilliant early morning sunlight. From the luxurious space in the bed he knew his wife had already risen. She would probably be preparing breakfast for his special day, his sixtieth birthday. As a young lad the anticipation of birthday cards and presents had always excited him, and even at sixty the expectation had not diminished.

He could hear the movements of his twin daughters in and out of the bathroom, rather subdued for a change. Usually the early morning atmosphere would be interspersed with high pitched argument of whose importance needed to be discharged first, or of uncontrollable laughter to which reason or circumstance he would never be privy. They were probably as much excited about their father's special day as he was.

As usual he held claim to the lesser portion of the duvet and his exposed feet had been abandoned to their fate, so to speak, which was six toes to each foot. He had once summoned up enough interest to delve into a medical dictionary to discover he was afflicted with Polydactyl, explained as 'autonomic dominated pattern of inheritance'. As this explanation did not encourage further probing he lost interest. The only drawback to having to accommodate six toes per foot was the need for wider shoes, which were more expensive, especially in the case of his bowling shoes.

Having been conscious for some twenty minutes he was surprised nothing had materialised. At the very least he surely had a right to expect breakfast in bed or a birthday card on his pillow from his beloved. They had to be plotting, waiting in mischievous delight in the kitchen. He put on his dressing gown and ambled into the bathroom, breathing in the heady aromas of mixed perfumes. He confronted his reflection in the mirror. Not bad for six decades he contemplated. He retained most of his hair, although the majority of it had turned silky white. Most of his teeth were intact and his eyes and ears still functioned without assistance. He bathed and shaved slowly and deliberately, then made his way downstairs full of expectations.

His wife appeared in the hallway, slipping into her coat and checking her hair in the mirror.

'You off already?' enquired Les, a little taken aback by her imminent departure.

Brenda glanced at him briefly, then back at her reflection. 'You've decided to get up then? Very gracious of you, I'm sure. I'm running fifteen minutes late. It's my day at the hospital. The girls have gone already. They're sitting their exams today.'

'But what about my . . .'

'You'll have to be firmer with them. They walk all over you. They've rushed in early to do some studying which you should have made them do last night instead of letting them go to that rugby club dinner. They were still singing rugby songs at well past midnight. Heaven knows what the neighbours will think! Who *was* Eskimo Nell anyway?'

'Eskimo Nell, eh?' grinned Les. 'That brings back some memories.'

'Well, you'll have to rely on your memory to get your own breakfast.'

'But it's my...'

'Yes, I know it's your own fault, lying in so late. Now think on – I've got a full day at the hospital library. Pushing that trolley around will play havoc with my legs. You'll have to get your own dinner as well. What are you supposed to be doing today anyway?'

Les stroked his chin thoughtfully. 'I'm down the bowls club this morning. I've got all the membership details to sort out as well as the green stewards' rotas to go through. I'm beginning to rue the day I volunteered to take over the secretary's job. It's a thankless task.'

'Well, just make sure you make a better job of it than Peter Morgan did. We never received our season tickets last year until halfway through the season: it was a ridiculous state of affairs. Now if you're going out, make sure you switch everything off and close all the windows. I'll see you later on.'

'But it's my birthday ... my sixtieth birthday...' But his half-hearted appeals were drowned out by the closing of the front door as his wife scurried down the garden path without a glimmer of a kiss, a wave or even a backward glance.

Deflated, Les consulted the calendar on the kitchen wall. Friday 5th October had been circled in red felt tip, but there was no indication that today was a special birthday. Clutching at straws he hoped that his cards and presents might be laid out in the lounge. A brief inspection dispelled this hope. Unbelievable! Dejected, he fixed himself some cereals and coffee. A nice fry-up would have been appreciated – not too much too ask on his birthday. He settled for toast and marmalade and a quick perusal of the morning paper. As usual it had been left open at the horoscopes; how could people believe all that mumbo jumbo? Out of curiosity he glanced at his own birthday sign. Libra.

'You may feel left out on an emotional limb, but luckily

Mercury will keep things on an even keel. Jupiter will do great things for your love life; just keep a clear vision of what you really want from a friend.'

Well, the first part might be accurate, but as for the second, fat chance! His love life of late had been flatter than the bank of England's interest rate.

Half an hour later he was pulling into the car park of the indoor bowls club. He noticed more than a dozen or so cars. The mixed triples league would be in full swing, just like grab a granny night on acid. At least at the club he felt appreciated. Club secretary was a very important position; so important he had held the post for two years now and couldn't get rid of it. Nobody wanted to know – a bit like his birthday really. Using his electronic key he entered the club and was immediately uplifted by the bright lights and the rich green carpets, complemented by the pristine white tops and smart grey trousers and skirts of the bowlers.

He passed along the rinks just as Mike 'Bomber' Harrison dropped one of his size six heavy woods onto the carpet with such force the thud reverberated around the hall.

'Hey, Mike!' protested Les. 'Watch the flipping carpet! You're not bombing Gerry today, the war is over.'

'Sorry, secretary sir,' grinned Mike, his big horse teeth gleaming under the lights. 'But look at all those short woods. How am I supposed to find a way through that lot? I might as well bowl overarm. And if that's not bad enough Elsie Whacket up the other end should be told not to sit there with her legs wide open. Not only is she putting me off, she's causing an echo.' Mike despatched his last wood up the green with such force it sent woods flying in all directions and the players running for cover. He turned round with an even bigger smile on his face. 'That's woke them up a bit; some of them were starting to nod off. You in the office today, Les?'

30

'Yes, for my sins. I've got a lot of work to catch up on.'

'Lucky devil! Don't think you'll be getting much work done. Gorgeous Gwen is on green steward's duty this morning.'

Les had hardly stepped into the office when Gwendolyn Payne jumped up from her chair, wrapped her more than ample body around him and kissed him full on the lips.

'Happy birthday, darling. Happy birthday.'

Les immediately felt both his spirits and his temperature rising. Gwen picked up an envelope from the desk and thrust it eagerly into his hands.

'Go on, open it up,' she said excitedly.

Les fingered the envelope, tracing his name accompanied by hand-drawn hearts and flowers. He slipped the card out and glimpsed the caricature of a large-breasted blonde lady with full red lips. He heard a click and a voice sang to him in husky sexual tones.

> Happy birthday to you!
> Happy birthday to you!
> Happy birthday, dear darling!
> Happy birthday to you!

'Do you like it? Do you like it? I chose it especially for you.' Gwen had the unique quality of instantly lighting up the whole room. A voluptuous woman in her late fifties, she possessed all the curves in the right places – just a hint more rounded, that's all. She wore a black frilled-collar blouse with the top buttons left undone to reveal more than a decent display of her ample bosom. Les pushed his face forward to give her a peck on the cheek but she deftly moved her head to receive the kiss full on her moist lips.

'Thanks a lot,' flustered Les. 'At least you've made my day; nobody else seems to have bothered. I was beginning to feel old and decrepit.'

'You're only as old as the woman you feel,' giggled Gwen, giving him another warm embrace. 'You don't look a day over fifty. Hasn't Brenda given you a card yet?'

'No, I think my wife has forgotten all about my birthday – too busy with her charity work. There was never a more ironic saying than "Charity begins at home". I even had to get my own breakfast.'

'Oh, you poor thing! Never mind, at least I didn't forget you. Now, Les, while you're in the office can I leave you to answer the phone? I've had a couple of strange calls this morning – somebody wanting to book a rink.'

'OK,' said Les, casually retrieving the new members' forms from the cabinet. He had hardly begun to sort through them when the phone rang. He half hoped it would be Brenda making her apologies.

'Langley Park Bowls Club, how can I help?'

'Ello, dis da bowls club?'

'Yes, secretary speaking.'

'Dis is Il Papa spicking.'

'Who?'

'Il Papa. You know, da bope from Italy.'

'Oh, I understand, the pope? Now what can I do for you. Your ... Holiness?'

'I wanna wish you a penis.'

'You what?'

'I say. I wanna wish you a penis.'

'You dirty little pervert!' shouted Les. 'What if my secretary had been on the phone?'

'I wanna wish her a penis as well, especially da ladies. I always wish dem a bigger a penis.'

'I bet you do, now get off the line. I've got your number. You just can't come on here spouting your filth!'

'What you talkin' about, da filth? I not speakin' da filth. I justa be polite an' wish you a penis. Justa like a Ken Dodd, you know: a penis, a penis.'

'Like Ken Dodd? Oh, I see what you mean, happiness, happiness?'

'Wassa da matter? You no speaka da Engleesh?'

'Yes, it's the accent that threw me. OK, you want to wish me happiness. Is there anything else you want?'

'Yes, I like a da give your secretary a big a penis as well.'

'I'm sure you would. Now, if there's nothing else, would you please get off the line.'

'I wanna book a da wink please.'

'You want to book a wink?'

'Yes, da wink you play da balls on. You Engleesh or bloody foreigner?'

Les shook his head in bewilderment. 'Now let's get this straight. You're the bope – sorry, the Pope – and you want to book a rink to play bowls on?'

'Dat's what I say, didn't I?'

'And when would you like this rink?'

'Tomorrow afternoon. Is pubic holiday in Italy? In da morning I give a da big blessing on da balcony, iffa da paint is dry. Two thousand of the nuns come to see me, da great Il Papa. I give a da special blessing; make a big a penis 'cos all da nuns are still da virgins. Then in the afternoon I polish my balls and come play on da wink.'

'There are no rinks available tomorrow afternoon,' explained Les.

'How you know?'

'I'm looking in da book. I mean *the* book.'

'What book? Da catholic book or the Church of England book?'

Les heard a distinct spitting sound at the mention of the second book. 'The bowls book, definitely no rinks available tomorrow afternoon.'

'Is not possible. Is pubic holiday tomorrow. I must have wink for afternoon.'

'Now listen. I've had enough of this nonsense. There are no rinks. R.I.N.K.S.F.'

A slight pause followed.

'Dere is no "f" in winks.'

'I know!' shouted Les. 'That's what I'm trying to tell you; there's no effing rink! Now get off the effing line!'

'Ah! You make a da joke. Il Papa like a da joke. I tell da nuns tomorrow.'

Les slammed the receiver down.

'Was that who I think it was?' enquired Gwen.

'Yes. Il Papa himself, wanting to book a wink.'

'You're lucky, I got Bill Clinton.'

'What did he want?'

'Wanted to know how long I was going to be on the blower.'

'What did you tell him?'

'I told him to go suck eggs.'

'Good for you.'

Gwen made some coffee and opened a packet of chocolate digestives. 'I shouldn't really but I'll just have the one.'

At 12.30 Gwen put the half-eaten packet of biscuits in the drawer.

'I've just seen Terry Ball pull into the car park. He's on duty until three o'clock. I just hope he's got his hearing aid turned on.'

Les looked up from his paperwork, somewhat disappointed that Gwen was leaving.

Gwen clipped shut her handbag and fluffed her hair up in the mirror. 'I fancy a spot of lunch, Les. What are you doing about dinner?'

'Nothing, I'm afraid. Brenda told me I would have to look after myself. Cast away like a piece of jetsam on my birthday.'

'What a shame! What a waste of your sixtieth birthday. I've got an idea. Why don't we go out somewhere? What about a nice pub lunch? I know just the place: The Rat and Ferret, out at Morley. It's nice and discreet out there. I'll drive, and then you can have a couple of drinks to celebrate your birthday.'

'Sounds very nice, Gwen, but I'm not sure Brenda would approve.'

'Of course she would. A spot of lunch and a couple of drinks. What's the harm in that between good friends? It's just unfortunate that she's busy on your birthday. She'll make it up to you later on, I'm sure.'

Les felt he capitulated a little too easily, but a pub lunch and a couple of beers appealed far more than cooking for himself. He hadn't visited The Rat and Ferret in years and they always carried a nice selection of guest ales, if he remembered correctly.

Terry Ball reported in for duty and studied the green stewards' book.

'Just what I wanted for a nice quiet afternoon. A Ladies' friendly!' His loose dentures rattled about like castanets. 'They'll be in here scraping about in their purses for five and ten pence pieces. It will take me all afternoon to count their green fees up. I see hairy Mary Carey's playing. That's all right – she usually brings in a bag of mint imperials. I'll see if I can scrounge a handful before she drops them all over the floor, like she normally does. Beth Harrington's playing as well, got a laugh like a fog horn. That should brighten up proceedings.' He looked up as Gwen and Les emerged from the inner office. 'Where are you two off to then? No hanky-panky, I hope?'

'If you must know, I'm taking Les out to lunch. It's his birthday.'

'You be gentle with him, Gwen. He's a married man, you understand. He won't be used to the close company of a merry widow. It's me you should be treating. I haven't had any excitement since Mavis Strong sat on my lap at the Christmas party. She very near broke my little cracker.'

35

'Get away with you,' said Gwen slipping into her cardigan. 'That's not what I heard when you accompanied Phyllis Green to Potters for a weekend of alleged bowling. The pair of you disappeared for three days.'

'Ah well, we spent most of the time sightseeing.'

'I bet you did, and I can imagine some of the sights you saw. Now listen on – if the phone rings and they don't give their name put the receiver down quick. We've been the target of some right nutters this morning.'

As they walked through the car park Gwen made sure she hung on to Les's arm. Les enjoyed the feeling; his wife very rarely did the same these days. Perhaps the excitement had drifted out of their marriage and he hadn't even noticed. Once in the car, he secretly admired her shapely legs. She was on the large size but she carried it well.

'Buckle up, Les, and hang on for dear life,' she laughed, manoeuvring out of the car park effortlessly. Her keen sense of anticipation helped her slip through the gears with silky smoothness and once on the open roads she wasn't afraid to open up the throttle. 'How am I doing?' she asked, smiling across at Les with her sparkling blue eyes and generous pouting lips.

'Well, you certainly don't take any prisoners, that's for sure.' He innocently patted her on the knee as she overtook two vehicles in quick succession. 'Fantastic! You should have been a rally driver.'

She slipped her hand over his. 'You haven't seen anything yet.' Then she rubbed his hand gently up and down her leg. 'You've got a nice touch, Les. Firm, but nice.'

At their destination, only a single parking space remained but Gwen reversed in and cut the engine all in one smooth movement. She picked up her handbag, then immediately dropped it into her lap.

'Bother! In my haste to get here I forgot to stop off at the cash machine and get some money out. I don't like using my card for small transactions. They soon build up and then I lose track of where I am. I never seem to have any money left over at the end of the month.'

'Don't worry about it, pet,' said Les reassuringly. 'Dinner is on me.'

Gwen leaned over and pecked him on the cheek. 'Oh, Les, you are a sweetie. It's hard to manage when you're on your own. People think it isn't but it is.'

She again held on tightly to him as they entered the pub. A few heads turned as the couple found a secluded table. An imitation fire glowed in the large fireplace and the subdued lighting presented a relaxed and romantic atmosphere. A sallow skinned waiter sauntered over bearing an unnecessarily large wine list.

'Not for me, Les. I don't usually drink at lunchtime. It doesn't agree with me; makes me go all light headed.'

'Go on, Gwen. It is my birthday. You can't leave me to drink all on my own.'

'Well, being as it's your birthday, but only if they have got a nice rosé. Couer de Grain Selle rosé is my favourite, but I don't suppose they stock it.'

The waiter's face beamed. 'I'm happy to inform you we do, madam. One of our finest wines, an excellent choice.' He pointed the wine out to Les at the bottom of the page. It was the most expensive of the rosés at £25 a bottle.

'A glass for the lady, please, and I'll have a pint of...'

'I'm sorry, sir. We only sell this wine by the bottle.'

Les flinched but quickly recovered. 'A bottle of the Couer de Grain Selle rosé and two glasses then.' The waiter bowed and swept away.

'This is nice isn't it, Les?' said Gwen helping herself to a breadstick from the centre of the table. 'I haven't been taken out for ages. Not that I'm very hungry. I'm more excited than hungry.'

The waiter returned and filled two generous sized glasses with a flourish. 'Will you be having starters?'

Gwen perused the menu while the waiter perused her cleavage. 'Not for me, Les. I very rarely eat starters, and then only salmon. It's so light on the palate. They don't appear to have any, so I think I'll pass.'

'You would have thought a place like this would have salmon,' commented Les, more relieved than disappointed.

The waiter bowed again. 'Madam. I understand it is not on the menu, but I do happen to know that we had a magnificent fresh salmon delivered this very morning. If you are not in any hurry I could personally ask the chef to conjure up some of his famous salmon *en croûte*.'

'Lovely,' replied Gwen, chomping on another breadstick and brushing the crumbs away from the corner of her mouth. 'As I said, I don't usually indulge in starters, but salmon is so light and low in calories you hardly know you've had it.'

Les settled for the whitebait and lemon vinaigrette, not quite the cheapest item on the menu but not far from it. He hoped Gwen would be choosing a salad for her main course. The expense was starting to mount up and if Brenda saw the statement he would have some explaining to do. But the wine was indeed excellent and he savoured his second glass with relish. The salmon turned out to be as sumptuous as promised and Gwen demolished it rather swiftly for someone not feeling particularly hungry.

The waiter hovered around the table again like a vulture.

'Can I suggest the chef's special for today? The stuffed medallions of pork. The stuffing is deliciously flavoured with peaches and fresh herbs and the pork comes from our highly recommended local suppliers. Delicate on the tongue and light on the figure.'

And no doubt hellishly expensive on the wallet, mused Les.

'Oh, would you believe it?' exclaimed Gwen, grabbing Les's hand in excitement. 'My absolute favourite! I can't bear to eat any meat other than pork. You will have some with me, Les. The stuffing sounds absolutely wonderful.' He felt her leg brushing against his in anticipation.

'Of course, darling. ' He returned the leg encounter with such force that the table wobbled.

'The vegetables are organically grown and freshly picked to complement the pork,' added the waiter, steadying the table and pouring the last of the wine into Les's empty glass.

'Leslie! You naughty boy, you've drunk all the wine. There's none left for me and it will go so well with the pork.'

'Another bottle, sir?' presumed the waiter.

The roast pork certainly turned out to be special and the apple sauce and accompanying vegetables were consumed in a flurry of flashing knives and forks. Gwen cleared her plate swiftly while Les struggled on, washing his meal down with two more glasses of wine. Gwen ordered a bottle of San Pellegrino to dilute her alcohol intake.

Les began to fancy that her voluptuous figure could be more readily explained by the practised way in which she devoured everything on her plate rather than her explanation of 'a slow metabolic rate'. He pushed his plate away and belched into his napkin. Gwen began to scan the sweet selection with far more enthusiasm than Les cared for.

'I don't usually have dessert,' she said.

'Good. I don't usually have dessert either,' slurred Les. 'There's no way I could manage a pudding.'

'Of course you can, big boy. You'll want to build up your strength for later on,' encouraged Gwen, beaming and thrusting out her bosom.

'Will I?' said Les, beginning to think this was his lucky day.

'As I say, I don't usually have dessert, but they've got

this fabulous *crème brûlée* with fresh fruits and sweet biscuits. It sounds naughty but nice – just like me.'

'Well ... er ... well, you go ahead,' said Les, his elbow slipping off the table.

Gwen eagerly followed his instructions and polished off her *crème brûlée* in five easy mouthfuls and with such zest he thought she might lick out the glass. For somebody who had claimed not to be particularly hungry or thirsty she had coped remarkably well.

'That was absolutely delicious, Les. I haven't been spoilt like this in a long time.'

'Coffee?' interrupted the waiter.

'No, definitely not,' replied Gwen.

Les breathed a sigh of relief. Gwen leaned across the table, her bosom growing more tantalising by the minute. She reached for Les's hand and stroked it enthusiastically.

'Now it's my turn to treat you.'

'It is?' stammered Les, swirling the last of his wine and swallowing it in one mouthful. He banged his glass clumsily down on the table.

'We'll have coffee back at my place. I want to show you my ... appreciation.'

'You ... d ... do?'

'Most certainly. You've got the afternoon free, haven't you? Free for some relaxation; and I've got a very nice bottle of brandy.'

Les's befuddled brain could conceive of nothing more pleasant. With help and guidance from Gwen he settled the bill and followed her outside to the car. Once inside, his head swimming and his body swaying, he leaned over to offer a kiss, but his blandishments were denied and she pushed him back into his seat.

'Now, Les, control yourself. Just be patient for a few more minutes.' Gwen made sure her amorous companion was securely strapped in before driving out of the car park.

Les absorbed the blur of the passing traffic. Smiling inwardly, he felt as light as a feather. He contemplated the delights to come, in the arms of a beautiful mysterious woman. A woman with only one thing on her mind: to show her appreciation for his generosity. Most men at the bowls club would give their right arm to be in his position. He thought of Brenda. but only fleetingly, the alcohol having banished any pangs of guilt. He knew he would never get the opportunity to be in this situation again. *Carpe diem*, seize the day. He didn't know exactly where Gwen lived but the leafy suburbs told him they were nearing their destination. With the gentle rolling of the car he could feel himself dropping off to sleep, but he willed his body to stay awake. Gwen smiled across at him and briefly stroked his leg.

'You are a handsome devil, you know. Fancy leading me on like this.'

Les could have sworn it was Gwen doing the leading but he couldn't care less. He vaguely remembered what the stars had predicted for his birthday: disappointment, followed by love and surprise. Perhaps there was something in this astrology lark after all.

They pulled slowly into their place of assignation. A quiet semi-detached bungalow, one of many in a cul-de-sac of neat lawns and freshly clipped bushes. Les admired his paramour as she moved her curvaceous frame effortlessly from her seat, her still-beautiful face surrounded by slightly greying hair, fashionably styled. She strolled purposefully to her front door – a woman on a mission – not for one moment caring if they were being watched by enquiring neighbours.

Les finally struggled out of his seatbelt and steadied himself before closing the door with enough violence to shatter the quiet of the afternoon. He patted the door in apology and put his fingers to his lips. 'Ooops a daisy!'

41

'Try and leave the door on its hinges, Les. I'm not particular about the neighbours, but no need to set the curtains twitching. It can be a bit like Peyton Place here at times.'

He followed Gwen, one hand reaching out for the wall for support. As she unlocked the front door and pushed it open the recently delivered mail fell onto the carpet. She stooped down to retrieve it, her ample buttocks stretching her black skirt to the limit. In his hurry, Les tripped over the doorstep and only managed to stop himself from falling by grabbing the nearest thing in front of him, those same amply curved buttocks.

Gwen broke into a fit of the giggles as she was propelled forward onto her knees.

'Bloody hell, Les! Let's at least get inside the house.'

Les mumbled his apologies, hardly knowing where to put his hands to gain support. She pushed open the lounge door and Les almost fell in. Gwen ushered her amorous suitor to a cream leather sofa festooned with so many cushions he scrambled about trying to find a place to sit.

'You'd better sit down before you fall down,' laughed Gwen.

Les slumped gratefully into the comfort of the material. He felt his body sink down low and the weight disappear from his unsteady legs. Gwen slipped his jacket off and hung it on the back of one of the dining room chairs. Taking this as an invitation, Les took off his tie and loosened his shirt.

'Is it me, or is it hot in here?'

Gwen tenderly ruffled his hair. 'I'll fix you that drink I promised. Now, think on – it's finest Napoleon brandy. You should savour it, not gulp it down like you did them two bottles of wine.' She switched on her CD player and the suave voice of Frank Sinatra began to croon gently.

'Strangers in the night, lovers at first sight…' The accompaniment of a rich string orchestra floated around the room from hidden speakers. She placed his drink on a glass coffee table and manoeuvred it to within arm's reach.

'Now, have I got a surprise for you?' As she leaned closer, Les thought her creamy white breasts would slip from their moorings. She murmured into his ear, her warm breath mingling with her heady perfume. 'I'm going into the bathroom to slip into something more comfortable. While I'm in there I want you to get yourself ready.'

Les attempted a feeble lunge at the shimmering breasts

but she slipped tantalisingly out of reach, crossed the room and closed the door behind her.

He sipped the brandy, took a deep breath and began to prepare himself. He unbuttoned his shirt and laid it carefully along the top of the sofa, only to see it slip and fall behind. At the third attempt he managed to stand up, unbuckle his belt and step out of his trousers. Casually he kicked off his shoes and, as he did so, caught a glimpse of himself in a mirror. The Y-fronts were clean but unflattering. He dispensed with them and they quickly joined the shirt behind the sofa. Now he was faced with a dilemma. Socks or no socks? That was the question. To any other red-blooded male it would be no socks, but insecurity about his polydactylic feet caught up with him. Would the shock of seeing six toes on each foot dampen her ardour? Would she draw back in horror? Too much of a risk. He decided to play safe and keep his socks on. He fell back onto the sofa struggling to get comfortable and at the same time look sexy. He pulled in his stomach and, just in time, spotted some fluff in his navel. He wheedled it out and secreted it under one of the cushions. Quickly, he took another sip of brandy. He heard the door handle moving. He lay there with outstretched arms.

'I'm all yours, my lovely,' he slurred.
The door slowly opened accompanied by giggling voices.

44

To the strains of 'Happy Birthday' a lighted cake was carried into the room by his two daughters, his wife Brenda and her best friend Gwendolyn.

3

Diary of an Angel

Hello, diary. My name, believe it or not, is Angela Angel. I have to admit that I was not placed on this earth as an angel. I arrived as Angela Verity Boocock. At twenty-one years of age I married George Reginald Angel. This is my diary for the year of Our Lord, 2004.

Saturday, 1 May

Little Tittersly Bowls Club is open for the new outdoor season. Must admit I am quite excited this year. Am determined to do well. Last season turned out to be most disappointing, with no medals, trophies or prestigious representative games to show for all my endeavours.

At the end of last season I entered my name down on lists for elected club captain, vice-captain, treasurer, secretary and social secretary. For all my enthusiasm I did not receive a single proposal or second for any of the aforementioned positions, though I know full well they were vacant. Refrained from putting my name down for club president as the stipulation is that you must have held some sort of office previously. How I am ever going to achieve my ambition of being a future club president is beyond me. Some joker put my name down as club toilet operative, but as nobody bothered to second, it was withdrawn. People

47

will have their fun. I consider myself to be above such misdemeanours.

I see Mr Russell Sprout is club treasurer this year. I do not trust him as his eyebrows meet in the middle and he has shifty eyes. There was a shortfall of £112.52 in the accounts last season, mainly down to old Mr Fotheringay, who is ninety-one and has been treasurer for as long as any one can remember. He was still using pounds, shillings and pence, having not yet got to grips with the decimal system.

When I arrived at the club, Mr Sprout informed me that the season ticket had increased in price from £60 to £62.50 and all club competitions by 50p each to £2. When I tried to explain that my incomings had not increased by twenty-five per cent, he told me to take it or leave it. He remarked that nobody was forcing me to enter every single competition. Have decided to give the Bagshot two woods and the target bowls a miss this season. They were my least productive competitions last year, when I failed to negotiate the first rounds against opposition I should have beaten with my eyes closed.

Made a small contribution to the Drake fellowship, but disappointed not to receive a miniature badge in recognition. Last year's badge depicted a bowler, and quite a jolly fellow he looked in my blazer lapel. However, after three weeks he went missing, presumed stolen, as I am always very careful with my equipment and accessories.

Entered my name for club singles, handicap singles, pairs, mixed pairs (drawn), handicap pairs (drawn), triples (drawn), mixed triples (drawn). Paid in advance for clubhouse locker, also to be drawn on Sunday 2nd May. Handed over £86.00 total in cash to Mr Sprout – who made a point of counting it three times and who made a big fuss of straightening out seventeen old five-pound notes I had diligently saved up in my flying pink pig. He didn't seem too impressed with the one pound in two pence pieces, but I informed him they all bore the sovereign's head and were perfectly legal tender. As a receipt didn't seem to be forthcoming – I stood my ground holding up a growing grumbling queue until I received said same.

Sunday, 2 May

Received an unexpected phone call from Nora Bell asking if I would like to be her partner in the open pairs. Agreed immediately, as Norah is quite a gifted player and has won many competitions. Glad to see my skill and professionalism is being recognised at last. Then she asked if I could pick her up at two o'clock so she could go down the clubhouse and sign on for the new season. Apparently, she has no transport since her husband, Ding-Dong, passed away in the middle of last season. Unfortunately, he suffered a heart attack helping newly widowed Dorothy Hardcastle 'decorate' her bedroom. I use the word 'decorate' in the loosest possible term. Who am I to judge?

I tried to explain to Norah it was a bit short notice and that I was in the middle of preparing Sunday lunch. I pointed out that the topside of beef I had purchased had failed to live up to its usual quality and needed an extra half hour in the oven. She seemed a trifle upset and declared that if it was too much trouble she would find another partner. Not wishing to lose out on an extremely good chance of winning a trophy, I promised I would pick her up at two o'clock prompt.

The ensuing roast lunch was not a great success and my dearest husband, George, complained that the meat was as tough as old boots, and he thinks he broke a crown on one of my roast potatoes. Then, to cap it all, I somehow managed to burn the apple crumble and the custard turned out lumpy. If I'm not careful, the pursuit of bowls perfection could well take over my life.

When I arrived, somewhat flushed and breathless, at Norah Bell's house she kept me waiting outside for fully half an hour while she enjoyed a glass of wine with her sister who had popped round 'on the off-chance'.

Eventually arrived at the clubhouse at 2.45 p.m. only to find all the free parking spaces taken. Had to fork out £1.50 for a minimum one hour stay. Extremely annoyed that Mrs Bell never had the decency even to open her purse.

While Norah sorted out her season ticket and competitions, I looked on the notice board to discover I had been allocated locker number twenty-four. Collected the key but disappointed to find out my locker was on the bottom row adjacent to the door to the gentlemen's toilet. While cleaning out the previous occupant's discarded chocolate wrappers, cigarette ends and unwanted lumps of chewing gum, noticed a rather pungent whiff escaping from the toilets.

Not only did I have all this to contend with, but whilst bending down had my behind pinched by at least two so-called gentlemen. I presume it was two; it could have been the same miscreant who did it on the way in and then again on the way out. When I complained to Mr Russell Sprout, club treasurer, he said I could take it or leave it as it was the only locker left.

On the way home, Mrs Bell casually asked if we could pop into Sainsbury's to pick up one or two items as she rarely had the opportunity to shop there now she had no transport. Told her this was fine as I needed some cold capsules and *The Sunday Times*. Most disappointed to find some petty thief had removed the supplement from my newspaper, and the capsules were temporarily out of stock. Mrs Bell checked out an hour later with a full trolley – so much for one or two items. Then, to crown it all, she had the cheek to ask me to load it into the boot as her back was playing up.

Monday, 3 May – Bank holiday

Enjoyed a nice lie in. Scrambled eggs on toast for breakfast. Husband George makes them wonderfully well with a dash of Worcester sauce. He, incidentally, remarked that mine always turn out like sponge rubber, which I thought a trifle unnecessary. Said he needed something light to settle his stomach after yesterday's lunch. Not one of my better ones, I have to admit.

George informed me that he would get cracking in the garden this afternoon, give the lawn its first cut and prepare the beds for the summer bedding plants. Offered to help, but he pointed out that, as I couldn't distinguish a weed from a wallflower, he would be better off on his own.

After a light lunch of rocket salad and pork pie slices, which unfortunately had holes in the middle where the egg should have been, went our separate ways. Spouse to his garden, and I down to Little Tittersly Bowls Club for a first roll up of the season. Dearest George bought me a pair of white leather bowling shoes for Christmas, and rather splendid they are. I thought I would look quite a picture on the greens in my freshly washed and ironed grey skirt, and my new white cardigan purchased in the January sales from Alsop's in the high street.

Arrived at the club to find everyone in good health and humour. Noticed that Nora Bell already playing in a pairs with Mrs Trotter, the new ladies' captain, Mrs Moores, ladies' club vice-captain, and Mrs Riddington, club social secretary. Most surprised not to have been invited to join them, but Norah has always been one to ingratiate herself with the hierarchy, while noticeably avoiding any responsibility. Everybody playing in pairs or triples so unable to join in just then. Didn't feel like playing on my own – makes one feel like a social outcast. Opening fixtures already up on the board. Put my name down for the first three matches. Feel quite confident will be included in all three.

Old Mary (Mother) Riley turned up, on her own as usual. Didn't really want to play with her as she is as deaf as a post, poor soul. Having a conversation with her is like talking to a foghorn. As I remember, ours went as follows:

'Do you fancy a roll up?'

'Who are you calling a trollop?'

'No, I said do you fancy a game.'

'Of course I'm glad I came. I am a member, you know.'

'Rink number eight is free. Shall we have a game?'

'No need to shout. I'm not deaf! If there's nobody else I suppose you'll do. Why don't we go on rink number eight?'

Mr Sprout already doing duties as green steward. There's something I don't like about him being in charge of money. Tried to charge me a green fee. Told him I was a member and didn't he remember me? It was only yesterday I signed on. Said he couldn't be expected to remember everybody and that if I had shown my card in the first place he wouldn't have to ask.

Helped Mrs Riley with her rather ancient bowls trolley down to rink number eight. Unfortunately, a wheel came off and pitched both Mary and her trolley into the ditch. After I helped her up she pushed me away and said it was all my fault for rushing her and that I should offer to pay to have the trolley repaired as she only had her old age pension with nothing left over for emergencies.

Discovered there were no mats and jack on rink number eight so I had to return to fetch them. Mr Sprout remarked that he could have told me they weren't out and I only had to ask. Insisted I pay a fifty pence cover charge on the jack. I am suspicious it's just another of his money making schemes.

Set the mat and jack up for Mrs Riley and had only played two ends when I noticed the club captain, Mrs Trotter, and her friends taking a keen interest in me. Perhaps she had me in mind for the town triples or rinks. After completing her end, she made her way over. Not an opportune time as I put a wood up on the wrong bias. She complimented me on my new shoes but explained they were the wrong colour and if I played in greys I had to have brown shoes like everybody else. When I informed her that they were the only pair I had with me she pointed out that I should read the rules. If she let me break them, other members would try and then chaos and anarchy would break out. Told her not to be so bloody stupid, which I instantly realised was a big mistake.

Endeavoured to explain to Mrs Riley that I needed to change my shoes.

'Screws? What do you want screws for?'

'Not screws, shoes!'

'What do you want screws in your shoes for? Never heard of such nonsense.' (I give up.)

When I told the green steward of my predicament he impatiently placed two boxes of second-hand shoes for me to sort through. Typical! Not one pair in size five, brown. Tried several in size four but all pinched. Had to settle for a pair of much worn and down-at-heel size sevens. I think they were an old pair of Mrs Hubbard's as she was overweight and had flat feet. Mr Sprout had the nerve to charge me one pound for footwear hire. When I protested he tried to snatch them back. Made sure he gave me a receipt. On returning to the greens, I tripped down the steps and laddered one of my tights at the knees. Heard somebody mutter, 'Pick your big feet up', which I decided to ignore.

When I reached rink number eight discovered old mother Riley had placed my bowls to one side and was playing with somebody else. I tried to explain that I was here first but she said she thought I had gone home and that she and Mrs Tremain had already started and that I would have to find another rink. No other rinks available. Stormed back to the clubhouse, threw the hideous hired shoes back at the green steward and returned home.

Arrived home in a foul mood. Threw my bowls bag in cupboard under the stairs and before George could open his mouth told him I would be retiring as I had one of my heads coming on. Lay on the bed with a damp flannel over my face and closed my eyes, only for George to restart the lawnmower. Threw the latest book I was reading, *How to Win Friends and Influence People*, at the window, missed and broke an antique china pot holding a bouquet of linen roses.

Thursday, 6 May

On the way to the shops to purchase a tube of superglue, I popped into the clubhouse to check if I had been picked for any of the opening games. Noted I had been selected as third reserve in both opening matches. Large underlined notice: 'All reserves to turn up. Important'. Team list for third match not yet selected, so decided to put my name down a second time just as a gentle reminder. On the way out noticed an envelope sellotaped to my locker. Quite elated, did not recognise the handwriting and presumed it must be one of the gentleman bowlers begging me to be his partner in the mixed pairs. Letter read as follows:

Dear Mrs Angel (membership No. 134),

The committee has decided to fine you a total of £5 for the following misdemeanours:

1. Swearing on the greens
2. Insulting ladies' captain
3. Throwing shoes at green steward/treasurer

Mr Sprout complained that he had been extremely shaken by the incident, but if an apology was forthcoming would not press civil charges. Both fines and apologies to be paid and made before exercising right to continue membership of club.

The committee.

Friday, 7 May

Waited until dearest husband George had gone to work, then sat down in filthy mood to write letter of apology. Have decided to put five pounds in a separate envelope addressed to the committee in case Mr Sprout claims he has not received same. I'm sure the treasurer has taken a dislike to me because I am watching him like a hawk as far as money is concerned. Noticed he was sporting a brand new club tie on Thursday. Hoped this was paid for at the going rate, or did he consider he deserved one as a perk of the job?

Dropped off both letters in letter box before club opened so as not to face anyone and to make sure my membership for Saturday's game against Victoria ladies would be valid.

Saturday, 8 May

Husband George enquired as to why the antique vase with linen roses now permanently glued to the window sill. Gave him one of my 'Haven't the faintest idea what you are talking about' looks.

Arrived at clubhouse at 1.45, regulation fifteen minutes before game due to start. Suffered the annoyance and embarrassment of being told by vice-captain, Mrs Ethel Moore, that to her knowledge I was temporarily banned from the club and shouldn't be here. Luckily, club captain Tilley Trotter arrived, rather breathless and with only ten minutes to spare (fine example to set to rest of club), to update the situation – viz. that fines having been paid and apologies accepted I was to be reinstated forthwith.

Sat for ten minutes in full bowling outfit defiantly displaying brand new white shoes. Informed that both teams one player short. First reserve promoted to play for Little Tittersly. Second reserve offered vacant position to fill in for Victoria ladies' and accepted. Alas, one of the tea ladies had gone A.W.O.L. and could I, as a goodwill gesture at being so swiftly reinstated, help out with the teas.

Studied the tea duty rota to discover would be assisting Patricia Willow, known as 'tit willow' behind her back, because of her enormous bosom. Have heard the tale that when she plays rinks she employs one of her old bras as a bowls carrier. I think this emanated from the gents' dressing room, so does not carry any weight – the story, not the bra. Patricia is a spinster with a wandering eye (not for members of the opposite sex, but her right eye has a mind of its own and usually rotates upwards towards the ceiling). Find it very difficult to look her in the eyes.

Patricia delegated herself to look after the kitchen – i.e. turn on the hot water urn and put teabags in seven teapots, six for the players and one for the travelling supporters. I was entrusted to arrange seven tables with eight chairs per table. Put on plastic cloths and cover these with white linen tablecloths, lay out eight cups and saucers with accompanying teaspoons and make sure sugar bowls and milk jugs full up. Bit of a one-sided affair really.

Old mother Riley – I'm sorry I must stop calling her that, Mary – turned up to help lay out the biscuits. I haven't forgiven her for abandoning me on the greens, but no sense in carrying on the feud. I feel it will start to get me a bad name in the club.

I noticed Mary laid out the biscuits in a very haphazard manner – i.e. one plate with fourteen ginger biscuits and two custard creams, the next table with thirteen wholemeal biscuits and only three Garibaldi, and so on. When I pointed out the unevenness of the distribution was told not to be an old fusspot. Noticed she had chocolate on her fingers and crumbs around her mouth.

Mr Russell Sprout doing green steward duty and in charge of money yet again. Not very happy about this. Gorged himself on four chocolate biscuits with his free cup of tea. Said he wholeheartedly accepted my apology and would I mind if he pinned it up on the notice board as a warning to other would-be miscreants. Then he had the nerve to ask if my old membership card was still valid or would I have to purchase another one. 'Old' indeed! I've only had it for eight days.

Missed out on a Victoria ladies' monogrammed bowls cloth presented as a 'thank you' to the tea ladies. Just my luck. Happened to be in the toilets helping to sponge down Mrs Daphne Divine's skirt and petticoat where she had spilled her tea. A very unusual woman, eighty if she's a day, almost completely bald, has only three fingers on her left hand and wears a G-string. For the life of me I can't think why.

Match result: Little Tittersly B.C. 104 points
Victoria Ladies' B.C. 125 points

I can only say serves the club right for leaving out one of their best players. After teas finished Mary Riley mysteriously disappeared. Tit Willow donned her bossy apron again and conveniently took care of the washing up, delegating me to clear all seven tables of crockery, used raffle tickets and biscuit crumbs. Task satisfactorily completed, broom and dust pan pushed out from kitchen for me to tidy up. I put on my jacket ready for home when the mop and bucket pushed out by unseen hands again from the kitchen.

'Mrs Willow, I have never seen the carpet mopped since I joined the club,' I protested.

'Don't be silly, Mrs Angel. It's for the toilets. Don't forget to give them toilet pans a good brushing, especially the gents'. Some of them are not too particular at what they leave behind.'

After a quick mop through I managed to escape to the relative fresh air and calm of the car park.

Husband George greeted me with a gentle kiss on the forehead. Noticed his nose wrinkle up.

'Enjoyed your afternoon, darling? Looks as though you worked up a bit of a sweat.'

'You could say that,' I mused, 'if you liked working as an unpaid skivvy.' Not quite what I had in mind at the beginning of the season.

Sunday, 9 May

Decided to give dearest husband, George, a treat of breakfast in bed. Two hard-boiled eggs, four halves of wholemeal toast, coffee, plus morning paper. Unfortunately, on descending stairs, tripped on hem of dressing gown and dropped the lot. Everything not lost though. Scraped two slices of toast off the wall and saved one egg from bouncing down all the stairs with a smart left-handed catch. Coffee ruined back page of newspaper so tore neatly off and disposed of it in waste bin.

After husband had finished in the bathroom he begged me not to experiment with new or exotic spices on his food without forewarning. Toast tasted of emulsion and boiled eggs not improved by additions reminiscent of carpet débris. Made a mental note that it would be his last breakfast in bed for the foreseeable future.

Wednesday, 12 May

Husband George to dentist to have crown repaired so popped into bowls club for a roll up. Greeted very warmly on the greens by the Rev. John Baptiste, retired Anglican minister.

'Ah, Mrs Angel. So nice to see you. The good Lord in his gracious mercy has delivered your virtuous soul to be my partner in the mixed pairs. When will you be free to participate in a practice session?'

'I'm free right now.'

'Ah, dear angel, the Lord is indeed a swift worker. I have never had the pleasure of working with an angel. Perhaps we can perform miracles between our bonded souls.'

'I do hope so, Reverend. I'll just go and change into my bowling shoes − brown, of course.'

When I returned to the green, the Rev. beseeched me to join him in a short prayer to thank the good Lord for sparing us through the night and for granting us a splendid new day ahead. Felt very self-conscious as this 'short prayer' lasted at least three minutes. Overheard some nearby children asking their parents if they could play statues also.

Commenced our practice session and after only two or three ends convinced our progress in the mixed pairs doomed to a short life. John Baptiste had the distinctive habit of crossing himself before delivering his woods and muttering, 'May the good Lord go with you'. Consequently, his woods sprayed far and wide, no doubt like his former church. After each end he put his arm around my waist and escorted me up the rink. Rather unnerving; even more so because of his insistence that I join him in singing the first two verses of 'Onward, Christian Soldiers'.

On the fifth end became quite scared out of my wits when he declared he would like to study me in what I thought he said was my missionary position. The very thought of him ogling me in my fragile sex life forced upon me such cold sweats that I've never experienced before. Somewhat relieved when he explained that my delivery position, not my missionary position, was in need of some divine intervention.

To help me with my imbalance on the mat he stood directly behind me, placing one hand around my waist and the other on my backside in an attempt to stop me, as he explained, from wriggling about at my moment of thrust.

I can assure you I felt very ill at ease, especially when a group of uncouth youths decided to have some fun at our expense.

'What's that bloke doing? Looks like he's going to give her one.'

'There's more to this game than what we thought!'

'Hey, Smiffy, didn't you know that Saga stands for "Sex And Games for the Aged"?'

'Shouldn't be allowed, all this pontificating in public.'

'It's pornification, you pillock!'

'Don't you pillock me. I'll smash your brains in!'

I saw this as my excuse to bring this disastrous practice session to a swift close. So I picked up my woods and hurried off, leaving the Rev. John Baptiste to deliver his eccentric brand of religion to the heathen band of hostile natives. I felt they were far more in need of conversion than me.

Arrived home just in time to answer the phone. Dearest husband sounded quite excited within himself. After having crown successfully repaired at the dentist he visited the travel agent to browse around. While doing so bumped into Samuel Sprocket, the deputy manager and an old golfing friend, who informed him that the bargain of the day was a half board holiday in Cyprus. A ten day vacation in the resort of Protaras had arisen owing to a cancellation through a sudden bereavement. This luxurious and very desirable holiday was going begging at half price, the only snag being the departure date was just six days away. Dearest thought the break might act as a wonderful relief to our stresses of the past month or so, his only concern being that it might clash with some of my forthcoming bowls matches. I must admit I couldn't understand what stresses he referred to, but spending ten joyous days lying in the sun or swimming in the warm blue waters of the Mediterranean was my idea of heaven.

Referring quickly to my diary found the only date of any consequence was the game against St Gilda's Bowls Club. I had put my name down for this ten rinker, but having been omitted from the first two games did not harbour any great expectations. 'Go ahead and book it, dearest George,' I almost pleaded. Kind soul enquired if absolutely sure and I confirmed, the only stipulation being that I might need a new swimsuit. He responded that such was my willingness to put my bowling career on hold he would throw in a matching sarong, sun hat and flip-flops.

Must admit that I held the line with bated breath. George came back on confirming holiday all booked and paid for from his last bonus. Decided to celebrate by running a hot bath and soaking in herbal mixture of Shea butter and almond blossom. Sheer heaven for both body and mind. Will recommend to dearest George to relieve his imaginary stresses.

Saturday, 15 May

Down to bowls club in my town attire of burnout blouse and matching cami top, complete with stone-coloured stretch trousers. Not a bowls accessory in sight. Some half a dozen or so people on the greens but of no concern to me. The club would have to manage as best it could without my services. Up to the notice board to strike my name from the St Gilda's match. Rather staggered to find team already picked and myself selected at number two on the captain's rink. (Oh dear! Oh dear!), my first proper match of the season. Talk about sod's law, if you'll excuse my French. Just to make matters worse, ladies' captain Mrs Trotter, accompanied by Norah Bell, entered the clubhouse just as I scratched my name from the list.

'Ah, Mrs Angel! Very encouraging to see you promptly initialling your place against St Gilda's. A very important match this, as I'm sure you realise. Nice to see such energetic and loyal support. There's too many malingerers and backsliders in this club.'

'I'm very sorry, Mrs Trotter...'

'No need to be. Anne, isn't it? I'll call you Anne from now on, if you don't mind. I've already forgotten about your misdemeanours of the past. A new start, shall we say? Your loyalty at filling in for the missing tealady has not gone unnoticed. You will find that such sacrifices will always be rewarded while I'm captain of this club. You'll also no doubt be pleased to know that, on the advice of Norah, you've been selected for two of the most important fixtures in the first month of the season.'

'I have?'

'Yes, indeed. Both great honours to be representing your club. If you glance across to the match board you'll see the dates. Make sure you initial these and put them down in your diary.'

Face to face with Mrs Trotter I found her quite a formidable lady, square set face and fierce brown eyes contrasting with her pale skin. With some trepidation I moved over to the board which, until now, had never once featured my name.

63

Town Ladies' Fours Competition, 23rd May

C. Plunket
A. Angel
N. Bell
T. Trotter (Capt.)
Reserves: A. Treemain. D. Riddington

Lady Hamilton cup v. Victoria Park, 26th May

Home	Away
A. Treemain.	A. Cockinmouth
A. Angel	E. Bygum
D. Riddinglon	N. Bell
T. Trotter (Capt.)	A. Moores (Vice-Capt.)

For a minute I thought I would fall through the floorboards; the next minute I wished I could.

'I'm sorry to have to . . .'

'Please don't harp on about being sorry, Anne. I've already told you that all is forgiven. Turn over a new leaf; a new era in your bowling career.'

'I'm sorry, Mrs Trotter, but I shall have to withdraw from the game against St Gilda's.'

'You what! But you've only just this minute initialled it!' said Mrs Trotter, her face aghast.

'No. I was in the process of scrubbing it out when you walked in.'

'Scrubbing it out? Just like that? Do you realise how much work and effort it involves selecting a team to play against St Gilda's? Ten full rinks leaves us with no reserves and you just saunter in and cross your name off. What if I hadn't just come in? Would you have erased your name and crept away with no explanation?'

'It's just not good enough – not good enough at all,' said Norah Bell, putting her two pennyworth in. I always thought Norah possessed a formidable nose. If I had to colour it, I think brown would be apt.

'And why can't you play? Have you broken a leg? Have you succumbed to some life-threatening illness?'

'I'm afraid I'll be on holiday.' I whimpered.

'You'll be on holiday! But it's only the first month of the season! You can't go on holiday the first month. It's unheard of. Besides, if I remember rightly, you put your name down on the match sheet not once but twice! Presumably so that I didn't overlook you the first time. Why in heaven's name did you put your name down if you knew you would be on holiday?'

'I didn't know at the time. My husband's only just booked it. He said it was a real bargain.'

'I bet he did. A real bargain, indeed. He'll have some bargaining to do with me the next time I set eyes on him. And how long will this holiday last?'

'Ten days.'

'Ten days? Heaven forbid! I don't get ten minutes' holiday throughout the season!'

Norah Bell mumbled sagaciously out of the corner of her mouth. Mrs Trotter exploded again.

'Well! That just about tops it all. You do realise this bargain holiday of yours will make you unavailable for the Town fours *and* the Lady Hamilton competition. Two of the most prestigious competitions of the summer?' Her face turned puce and she tore down the team sheets with such ferocity I thought she would do herself some injury. 'I just don't know why I bother, I really don't.'

As I shuffled shamefaced to the door, Norah Bell waved a warning finger at me. 'I shall have to find myself another partner for the pairs. You're not reliable enough, not reliable enough at all.'

Tuesday, 19 May

Depart at 10.00 a.m. for Gatwick airport to catch flight BX 104 to Larnaca for ten stress-free, and bowls-free, days' holiday.

Am seriously thinking of taking up tiddly-winks on my return.

4

Young Blood and Old Bones

The sun beat down out of a cloudless azure sky, its unrelenting rays turning the manicured grass paler by the hour. A cordon of orange and yellow rose bushes, interspersed with pink hydrangeas and blood-red rhododendrons, surrounded the picturesque bowling green. Mother Nature had generously provided the perfect afternoon for a game of bowls. From the cover of the largest rhododendron bush an old man stood watching, waiting, and concentrating deeply.

Tom Atherton's face was long and lean and set on a neck as pink as a rhubarb stalk. His dancing eyes showed flecks of red in the corners. He shaded them with his hand while observing the lone bowler on rink number three. He studied this meticulous individual who despatched woods up and down the green with measured authority. Each wood finished its journey no more than a foot away from the yellow jack. Several of the woods gently nudged the jack first one way and then the other.

Tom's instincts told him that the bowler was good, very good. No doubt practising for a forthcoming game of some importance. Tom reckoned he could take him. Sure he could take him, not a shadow of a doubt.

On the green, the sultry heat caused the head of Curtis Youngblood to perspire so much that his heavily pomaded hair lay flat against his scalp as if made of patent leather.

His white shirt could have been torn straight from its cellophane wrapper and his immaculately tailored grey trousers possessed a crease so sharp he was in danger of doing himself an injury. The unblemished reflection in his brown bowling shoes mirrored the self-satisfied smile as his final wood nestled against the jack.

The squeaking iron gate barely disturbed his concentration, but the clattering of a string bag of bowls being deposited on the green caused him to curse under his breath. He turned to witness an ungainly figure slowly manoeuvring its frail body over the low iron railings which surrounded the greens.

'Gee! Never seen bowling as pretty as that in all my days. Pretty as a picture. No wonder you're playing all on your lonesome. Shouldn't be surprised there's nobody to touch you in these parts.' Tom clapped his hands in appreciation.

Youngblood did not particularly care for the uninvited intrusion on his leisure of this rag-tag of a fellow standing in front of him. He took in the battered canvas shoes and the ill-fitting trousers. The off-white jumper that hung from his scrawny shoulders resembled a shroud. To Youngblood's dismay life appeared in the old body. It held out a surprisingly delicate hand with long, tapering fingers and polished nails.

'Pleased to meet you. Tom's the name, Tom Atherton. I'm over here on a month's vacation from the United States.' He glanced with admiration at the woods, the sun's rays bouncing off them like eels skipping about in shallow water. 'Sure are some fancy looking woods. I bet you a dollar to a dime you're some sort of county player?'

'Well, I have had a couple of games...' But before Youngblood could finish his sentence the old man performed a celebratory jig with such enthusiasm he stumbled into Youngblood.

'I just knew it, just dang knew it. Ooops! Not too steady on the old legs these days.'

Youngblood's eyes and shoulders narrowed. 'You're American then? Don't get many of you on our bowling greens.'

'No, no, I'm not a damn Yankee,' replied Tom in disgust. 'I'm English through and through. Born and bred in the county of Yorkshire. Married a sweet girl from Memphis, Tennessee, over thirty years ago. She's been dragging me around the States like a dog on a leash ever since. I'm on a month's vacation to visit with my kith and kin while there's still a flicker of life in this old body of mine.' He tipped his set of dull battered woods onto the grass. 'Care to give an old feller a game?'

'Actually, I was just finishing off,' muttered Youngblood, not wanting to be seen with this refugee from an Oxfam shop. A pair of warblers darted out of a hawthorn tree. The two men watched in admiration as they zigzagged away over the municipal gardens to the cooler refuge of the river bank.

'Aw, go on, make my day,' pleaded Tom. 'Make my day to say I played on the same rink as an actual county player. Something to tell the folks back home in Tennessee. Just a couple of ends or so?'

Youngblood glanced briefly at his gold-plated watch. 'All

right then, as you are all the way over from the States. He placed the mat and swiftly rolled up a full length jack. He stepped off the mat. 'After you.'

'No sir, after you, I insist,' offered Tom in his southern drawl. 'I need you to remind me how to play this dog-gone game. We usually have ten big skittles to aim at back home.'

Youngblood sent his first wood up to finish a foot from the jack. Tom picked out a wood and turned it carefully over in his hands.

'These balls are so old I can hardly tell which is the biaas any more.'

'It's called the bias.'

'The bias then. Not that it matters much. My old pop used them until he was eighty-four. Plumb worn out they are, just like me.' He bumped his first wood up on the backhand, the curve running ever wider until it finished on the adjoining rink.

'Jeez, still must have got the bias back to front.'

With the end completed Youngblood finished with four shots, all within two feet of the jack. Tom's feeble endeavours ended with a wood on each adjoining rink and the remaining two barely halfway up the rink.

'Sure is pretty, pretty as a picture,' complimented Tom, surveying the winning woods. 'Never could get the hang of this game.' He scratched the few wisps of lifeless hair at the side of his head. 'Know what's missing? I gotta have something to get me fired up. A little wager or something. How about the first one to score eleven for ten bucks?'

'Bucks?' said Youngblood, fingering the diamond and gold ring on his little finger.

'I do believe I mean pounds. Come on, you're already holding four shots.'

'I can't play you for that sort of money,' replied

Youngblood, rolling up another toucher. 'It wouldn't be fair.'

'Who's talking about fair? You're giving an old feller the excitement of his life. You win and I'll gladly give you ten dollars – sorry, pounds. That's the least I can do for walking on the same green as you. You lose and you owe me nothing. Can't be fairer than that.'

The second end finished the same as the first: four shots to Youngblood. The three needed to win the game were picked up without trouble on the third end.

'Beautiful bowling,' praised Tom, shaking his opponent's hand and slapping him several times on the back. 'Tell you something, mister, you lived back home in the States you could sure make yourself a whole heap of money. Give me the pleasure of another game and I'll double the stakes.'

Youngblood appeared mesmerised by the easiest ten pounds he had ever earned. He was equally excited about the prospect of doubling it.

'What? Same conditions and no complaints if you lose?'

'Sure thing, pardner,' smiled Tom. He scrutinised his opponent through half-closed eyes which gave his face an even more haggard look. He slipped a silver hip flask out of his back pocket and unscrewed the cap. 'Care for a quick snort? It's hotter out here than the middle of the Nevada desert.' Youngblood declined the offer. Tom took a couple of eager swallows.

'Pure Tennessee rye whiskey. Shouldn't myself really. Don't do my focusing any good at all.'

Halfway through the second game Tom accidentally tripped over one of his woods and fell at Youngblood's feet. Tom hardly had the strength to stand up. Youngblood hauled him up and steadied him. 'You all right, old feller?'

'Yeah, yeah, I'm okay. Told you I shouldn't drink that whiskey; be the death of me.' He pushed his opponent away. 'I'm fine, I'm fine.'

Youngblood drilled his last wood up the green and carefully studied its progress, when the old man suddenly became agitated.

'Look out! Look out! There's a snake!'

Youngblood glanced around to see Tom dancing around and pointing to the ground. That sure must be some firewater the old boy was drinking.

'Snake? What are you talking about?'

'Down by your left foot. I wouldn't move if I was you.'

Youngblood looked down at his left foot and couldn't believe his eyes. 'How the devil did that come out? It's not a snake, you old fool, it's my shoelace.'

'Your shoelace? From back here it looked like a Tennessee Tiger. Pesky varmints can give you a nasty bite, make your foot swell up twice its size. I better lay off this whiskey, tastes more like moonshine in this heat.'

The second game finished as the first had done, with an eleven shots to nil result. 'If only I had my camera,' sighed Tom appreciatively. 'Been carrying it around with me all week. Now, when I need it, I haven't got the dang thing. Takes pretty pictures, too.' He took out his wallet and fingered a twenty pound note.' I don't suppose you'll do me one last favour? You've been a real gent to me this afternoon. Give me one final go and we'll round it up to fifty pounds.'

Youngblood's eyes widened in disbelief. 'But fifty pounds is a lot of money.'

'Now don't you go worrying about the money. I know I'm not going to live long enough to spend all the money I've got, and I sure as hell don't want to hand it over to the tax man.' He took two more gulps from the flask. 'Tell you what. I'll even play left-handed just to give you the edge.'

'All right then, fifty pounds it is, but definitely the last game.'

A group of club members, some carrying their woods, and some pulling them along in trolleys strolled leisurely up to the railings.

'What's going on here then, Curtis? You playing with old father time?'

'Better hurry things up. Looks like the old feller's on his last legs.'

Youngblood sidled over to his cronies. 'You won't believe it, but this old duffer insists on playing for money. He already owes me twenty notes. Now he wants to up the stakes to fifty.'

His friends offered their encouragement.

'Take it, if he's throwing it away.'

'Yes, and we'll be in the bar waiting.'

'It will be doubles all round,' laughed Youngblood. 'The old coot's not had a shot within a yard of the jack.'

With one wood left to play on the first end Youngblood held four shots, two either side of the jack. Tom had overplayed and all three of his woods had finished some two yards through the head. He bounced his last wood with such force it left a visible indentation in the turf. Youngblood closed his eyes in disgust. When he opened them it was to see the bowl squeeze in between his four, pick up the jack and rest it close to Tom's three back woods.

Tom hurried up the green as fast as his skinny legs could carry him. He hooped and hollered. 'I do believe I've got myself a full house!'

The spectators sniggered amongst themselves. Youngblood shook his head in disbelief.

Still excited by his stroke of luck, Tom threw down the mat and put up a three quarter length jack. His first wood finished perfectly in line but a yard short. Youngblood's first attempt bumped his opponent's wood closer to the jack before screwing away. Exactly the same thing happened with the remaining woods. In trying to push them out,

Youngblood only succeeded in pushing them closer. The old man executed another of his celebratory jigs.

'You're a real gent, knocking me in for another full house. Didn't realise I've been playing with the wrong hand all the time. No wonder I've never won a dang thing.'

The spectators' interest broke out into earnest encouragement. Several could see the promise of a free drink disappearing.

'Come on, Youngblood. Stop messing about!'

'Surely you're not going to let old Methuselah take you for a sucker?'

Youngblood felt the searing heat burn the back of his neck. He swatted away a bunch of midges. Things were not going to plan. Tom Atherton licked his fingers and rolled up a long jack. His first wood pushed the jack into the ditch and toppled in along side it.

'Glory be! Glory be! May the good Lord be praised!' exclaimed Tom, sinking to his knees. Youngblood felt obliged to help the old man to his feet again.

'Well bowled. I'm beginning to think you've played this game before.'

'Nope, I swear I haven't played in forty years. May the good Lord strike me down.'

Youngblood sighed in despair. He couldn't win the end, but he needn't lose the game. It was damage limitation time. He felt the sweat run down his brow and drip off the end of his nose. He brushed it away and blinked into the sun. To his relief his first attempt finished only a foot from the edge of the rink. It drew generous applause. Tom obliged by knocking the wood into the ditch and leaving his own in its place. When he did exactly the same with his third and fourth woods he turned around so quickly he bumped into Youngblood reaching for his final wood.

'Gee, I'm so sorry. I'm so excited I don't know what I'm a doing of.'

'Calm down, it's not over yet,' said Youngblood.

'Sorry. But I just know you're going to draw the second shot. I just know it.'

Youngblood composed himself. He knew exactly what to do with his last wood. Just tip any wood over the edge and he would pick up second or third shot. His hands felt wet and sticky. The relentless sun blazed directly into his eyes. He summoned all his concentration. At the crucial moment of delivery two things happened. First his trousers fell down and, in utter astonishment, he let the wood slip from his grasp.

He couldn't decide which predicament was the worst to comprehend. The sight of his trousers round his ankles or the sight of his wood coming to a perfunctory stop halfway up the green. He heard the laughter of the spectators getting louder and louder as they realised what had happened.

'You see that? His trousers fell down.'

'Talk about getting caught with your pants down.'

Youngblood quickly pulled up his trousers to cover his embarrassment. How could his trousers just fall down? He turned around to find the reason why. His leather belt lay on the grass two feet from the mat. Tom was a couple of yards further back, leaning against the railings and treating himself to another quick snort from his hip flask.

'Well, that was the dangest thing I ever did see, you gone and dropped your breeches.'

Youngblood was not amused; he stormed up green, threw his woods into his bag and hurried off to the clubhouse.

'Hey feller! Haven't you forgotten something?' yelled Tom. 'I do believe you owe me fifty bucks.'

Youngblood turned around, his face as black as thunder. 'But you said I wouldn't owe you anything if I lost,' he stammered.

'Yeah, sure enough on the first two games. I don't recall saying anything about it on the last game. Seems to me, if I'm willing to pay up on my two losing games, you should pay up on yours. Any southern gentleman would have the decency to do that much.'

'Well, I'm not one of your so-called southern gentlemen,' cursed Youngblood, hastening off the green.

Tom picked up his woods, shrugged his shoulders and winked at the spectators. 'Some you win, some you lose.'

In the clubhouse Youngblood approached the bar, badly in need of a drink. 'Did you see that con man out there? Trying to fiddle me out of fifty quid. He'll have to get up early in the morning to catch me. I bet he was no more American than my ex mother-in-law. Pint of the best, John. My mouth's as dry as sandpaper.'

'Pint of the best coming up.'

'Hope you can change a twenty. The cash machine didn't have any tens.'

'Shouldn't be a problem,' said the barman.

But it was a problem, a very big problem, because when Youngblood opened his wallet all he found in his money pocket was a brown shoelace. He stared in astonishment at his shoes. Both laces were missing. He knew he had one in his pocket which had come out on the green, but how did the other finish up in his wallet? He turned his wallet inside out.

'All my money's gone! I drew five twenties out this morning. I know I had a hundred pounds!'

He desperately searched his pockets – nothing but the other shoelace. His face turned as white as the patches on his wrist and little finger where his gold watch and diamond ring had been. Finally, the proverbial penny dropped. He'd been turned over good and proper. He dashed to the door and looked over to the far green where they had been playing but the old man was gone, long gone.

5

I Don't Know Whether to Kill Myself or Go Bowling

Fraser Woodcock gazed at his ageing reflection in the bathroom mirror and wished the bruising and discoloration would hurry up and disappear. Perhaps some of the foundation make-up his wife used would help. His finger inquisitively traced the small print on one of the many pots lined up on the glass shelf. 'Improves the appearance of fine lines and wrinkles, for a flawless finish and a younger, fabulous look.' Possibly a bit late in the day for that he thought.

'I'm ready for my hobnobs now, pet.' Betty's voice lilted in pleasantly from the bedroom. Fraser gently towelled his tender face, turned out the light and shuffled through to the kitchen. He poured the coffee into Betty's favourite mug, the pink one with 'The best wifey in the world' motto. He slipped the biscuits out of the packet on to a rose-covered plate, placed them on the tray and carried it carefully into the bedroom.

'You're looking a bit pensive today, dear,' commented Betty, her eyes detecting the slight nervousness in his movements. Fraser lovingly returned the smile. Her hair was now short and grey, whereas it had once been long and blonde, her brow slightly lined where it had been as smooth as silk, but her eyes had lost none of their beauty and sparkle.

79

'I've been summoned to the clubhouse for an emergency committee meeting,' Fraser reluctantly informed her.

'Summoned? Oh dear. I did warn you about taking on the post of acting treasurer.'

'I'm afraid I've done something very silly and it looks as if I've been found out,' replied Fraser, rolling his tongue over dry lips and avoiding Betty's inquisitive eyes. 'It could get me thrown out.'

Betty carefully dipped a biscuit into her coffee. 'There's plenty of other bowls clubs,' she observed dismissively. 'You're not a bad man, Fraser – impetuous and foolhardy at times, but not bad.'

'If push comes to shove it could get the club thrown out of the clubhouse.'

Fraser opened the curtains and watched the sunlight dance fleetingly through the sycamores on the far side of the street. From under the pillow Betty handed Fraser a slip of paper; he studied the frail writing.

'"Red Hot Tomato" and "A Bag of Nuts". That all?'

'That's what I fancy today, thank you.'

'I'd better pop into the shop on the way to the clubhouse then. It could be a long meeting.'

He plumped up her pillows and tucked the duvet around her. He knew that as soon as he left the house she would spend the rest of the morning in bed, first with Terry and later with Bruce. They were her regulars. Fraser was not a jealous man; after all, she still had her needs. He passed over the portable radio. 'I've tuned it in ready for you. Terry Wogan will be on in ten minutes, followed by Brucey. Enjoy your morning darling.'

Betty blew a lingering kiss and he managed to blink away a tear. The sight of his bedridden wife brought a lump to his throat which got harder to swallow each day.

After breakfast Fraser slipped into a clean white shirt and grey slacks. He wrestled with his club tie in the hall

80

mirror. The facial damage glared angrily back at him; it would take some explaining to the committee members. The club badge on his blazer bore the motto, 'To Trust and Serve'. He felt he had failed miserably on both counts. He scooped up a handful of betting slips from the hall table. Perhaps if he doubled the stake money their luck would change.

In the furtive depths of the smoke-filled betting shop, Fraser wrote out two slips. The first, a one pound win on 'Red Hot Tomato' in the 3.30 at Lingfield. The second, a one pound win on 'A Bag of Nuts' – red hot favourite in the big handicap at Newmarket. As he handed over the stake money, a firm hand descended accusingly on his shoulder.

'Caught you red handed!' a triumphant voice boomed. 'Spending all the club's much needed funds on three-legged nags!'

Fraser winced, but quickly recovered as the offensive smell of stale tobacco and even staler whiskey fumes wafted from Fred 'Stonky' Jones.

Fraser smiled weakly at a character who enjoyed bad teeth, bad breath and a complexion red and puffy from too much alcohol. Apart from that he was a useful little bowler who enjoyed nothing more than cocking a snook at club officialdom.

'Hello, Stonky. Just putting the wife's little flutter on – one of the few pleasures left to her these days.'

Stonky's face cracked into an amiable grin. 'How is the old girl these days? Not in too much pain, I hope? Sure miss her down at the club; not the same without her. Life and soul of the party.'

Fraser glanced up at the clock. 'She's bearing up, Stonky. Thanks for asking. Sorry, must dash. There's an emergency committee meeting at the clubhouse.'

Stonky's bloodshot eyes widened. 'Heard there was a bit

of a stink going down. Hope you haven't blown all the club funds on slow horses and fast women.' His raucous laugh gained the immediate attention of everybody in the shop.

The drive out of town to the Valley Bowls Club was carried out more or less on automatic pilot, his mind sifting over the financial mess the club found itself in. He pulled up alongside other members' cars, his self confidence draining away. Through the window he saw members were already seated around the table. Their conspiratorial conversation ceased abruptly as he dragged out the vacant chair and fought against the nausea in the pit of his stomach. Opposite him Colonel Barnes-Rose, President and life member, thoughtfully stroked his clipped silver moustache and set a gold framed monocle in his left eye. Under the table he wriggled his right foot, the dreaded gout playing up again as it always did when he became agitated.

'Let us begin by stating the facts plainly, as I see them.' He paused for effect. The Colonel was nothing if not dramatic and curt in all his dealings with men serving under him. 'The club funds under your inept management have mysteriously plummeted from a healthy one thousand two hundred and fifty pounds, to a mere one pound, fifty-three pence. Hardly enough to keep the club in postage stamps. Where the devil has all the money gone to, Woodcock?'

Fraser tried to moisten his lips but his tongue resembled coarse sandpaper. He partially opened his briefcase as if to present documents and receipts to account for the steep decline in fortune, but a less impressive sight greeted his eyes: a dozen or so failed betting slips, outdated lottery tickets and four red-lettered final demands – one each for electricity, water and sewage and, more importantly, one from the local council for rent and rates on the clubhouse. He clicked the briefcase shut, wriggled back the chair and commenced his defence.

'I'm afraid we are suffering from what could be called a bit of a cashflow problem. I can assure you it is only temporary and nothing to get upset about.'

'Nothing to get upset about?' spluttered Colonel Barnes-Rose. 'I don't suppose this threat of eviction the club secretary received this very morning is anything to get upset about either?' questioned the Colonel, waving the threatening piece of paper in the air as if it were a proclamation from the Queen herself. 'I repeat the question: where has the money gone?' A murmur of support rumbled from the ranks of the Colonel's cronies.

'I lent the money to somebody.' Even Fraser himself appeared dismayed and disgusted at the pathetic explanation he offered as his second line of defence. Grasping at any straw that might suggest a genuine excuse, he added, 'I lent the money to someone who could have been highly embarrassed if unable to stump up the necessary at short notice.' Fraser paused and gasped for breath. 'I think, gentlemen, that you will find the club's financial clout has been put to true humanitarian needs.'

The Colonel blinked in astonishment.

'You actually mean you lent the club's private funds to an individual? But you had no right, man. It's not your money. We are not in the business of making financial loans.' He waved his hands in despair. 'I demand to know whom you lent it to, when we can expect the money back and at what rate of interest.'

The rest of the committee grumbled among themselves, casting accusing glances at the pathetic figure facing them, a man who had bought their ancient and beloved club to the brink of financial ruin. Fraser avoided their eyes and allowed his gaze to flicker across the various pennants that adorned the hallowed walls. Perhaps divine inspiration would be his saviour. His eyes settled on the 'Drake Fellowship' collection box. No hope there; he had pillaged that very container a week ago. Twenty-seven pence, two brass blazer buttons and the remains of an extra-strong peppermint had been its paltry contents.

'I'm sorry, but I cannot name the individual on grounds of confidentiality. All I am prepared to say is that it concerns a very highly respected member of this club who has promised me that, as soon as she is released from hospital, she will return the money.' This explanation prompted a further spate of mutterings.

'Who have we get in hospital?'

'A member of the ladies' section?'

'Vice-Captain Maud Belcher is in hospital. My wife has temporarily taken over her duties.'

'Ah, the Bearded Lady,' chuckled Tom Simpkins, stroking his chin in playful muse.

'That's enough!' remonstrated the Colonel. 'If it is Maud Belcher, well, she's a damn fine woman. Founder member of the ladies' section and all that. However, I was under the impression we had had a collection for her. I remember putting a fiver in it myself. Who organised the whip-round?'

'I'm afraid it was Fraser, sir,' whispered the secretary.

'Goddam it, man. Have you got your sticky fingers into everything?' His waving hand calmed further accusations that began rippling around the table. 'Must be embarrassing for the poor woman, but I'm sure our money is safe with her. We will just have to think of a way of stalling the council.'

At last, Fraser felt able to offer some good news.

'Maud has promised half the money back at the weekend. As far as I understand, she entered the hospital for a course of six treatments to remove excess facial and body hair. Unfortunately, the operations have not gone as well as expected so she has cancelled the last three and demanded half the money back immediately. The latest news I have is that she intends to keep the beard, but at least now she can display her bosom in public.' Fraser paused briefly. 'I am sure Maud will show her appreciation to everybody when things return to normal. Especially to you, Colonel, as I do believe the lady has a soft spot for you'.

'Should be a helluva lot softer now,' chuckled Tom Simpkins.

'That's enough!' warned the Colonel. 'I think we should draw a line under this particular episode for the time being.'

Fraser closed his eyes and allowed himself the luxury of a few deep breaths. Sailing close to the wind did nothing for his erratic heartbeat. He pushed back his chair and began offering his goodbyes. The committee were not that bad after all, he thought – only doing their job.

'Sit down, Fraser! We haven't finished yet,' ordered Colonel Barnes-Rose, fiddling with his collar as if a jet of steam were about to issue from his neck. With practised dexterity, he slipped open the top of a large manila envelope and unfolded two pages of pristine typescript. 'Do you know what we have here, Mr Woodcock?'

'I'm afraid you have the better of me, Colonel.'

'This is an official complaint, the first I've received, I'm sorry to say, during my tenure of presidency. It comes, registered post, from the captain of Netley-on-Sop Bowls and Croquet Club. It involves an incident which occurred in the cup match against them last week. Does anything spring to mind?'

Fraser suddenly felt the minor bumps and weals on his face double in size and colour. They took on the throbbing of a small turbine pumping station.

'Er, not immediately. I know we gave them a damn good thrashing. Bad losers that lot, always moaning'.

'It's got nothing to do with winning or losing and, if there's any truth in the matter, it's you who deserves a damn good thrashing. The complaint is specifically from Miss R. Soul.'

Tom Simpkins doubled over in hysterics and banged his head on the table. Several stifled chuckles escaped from other committee members.

'This is not a laughing matter!' insisted the Colonel, his monocle dropping out in indignation. 'Miss Rosemary Soul, to give her full name, has lodged a complaint that she was assaulted and interfered with on two separate occasions during the match. She adds further that she was so stung by shame and humiliation she found it necessary to slap her opposing number two firmly across the face on both occasions. We've checked this out and, according to the team sheets, you were the said opposing number two.'

Fraser's face crumpled from an expression of forlorn embarrassment to one of abject misery. The nightmare incidents flashed across his brain.

'I see by your expression it rings a bell,' the Colonel observed drily.

'It was nothing – a complete misunderstanding,' offered Fraser.

The Colonel's face gradually turned crimson. 'It appears your actions lately are littered with misunderstandings. The captain of Netley-on-Sop vouched for the impeccable character of Miss Soul. Member of the church choir, leading light in the Women's Institute. She goes on to state in no uncertain terms that unless she receives a full and unequivocal apology from both you and the club, she will have no hesitation in taking the matter further by placing it in the hands of her solicitors. Which makes it extremely awkward because the same firm of solicitors generously provide a large sponsorship to this club.' The quivering monocle dropped once again from an intense countenance. 'Good god, man! What on earth did you do to the poor woman? Not only are you determined to bankrupt the club, we could well be dragged before the courts on assault and battery charges!'

More groans and shaking of heads spread among the assembled members. Eyes full of menace glowered at the abject figure fidgeting before them. Fraser Woodcock trembled as he painfully recalled the incident.

'It's all been blown up out of proportion.'

' "Blown up" isn't the word, "erupted" seems more apt. Now tell us exactly what happened.'

'As I recall, she was playing number two for Netley. The incident occurred after about ten ends. If you remember, the afternoon was extremely hot and sultry. It didn't take much of an effort to break out into a sweat. Well, this lady played the second of her two shots – a damn good shot too, picking up the jack and turning our one shot lead into a two shot deficit...'

'Fraser! Get on with it, man. We can do without the ball-by-ball running commentary.'

'Well, as I say, she had completed her second shot and was standing back admiring her handiwork when I noticed her white bowls skirt, which appeared to be made out of extremely flimsy material, had unfortunately become ... er ... wedged in ... er...'

'Get on with it!' ordered the Colonel impatiently. 'It's no good having second thoughts about it now. You should have done that on the day in question.'

Fraser stroked a shaking hand across a furrowed brow.

'It had become wedged in ... er ... the cleft of her ... er ... buttocks.'

'Buttocks?'

'Well, I thought it looked very unsightly and she, being obviously engrossed in her successful delivery, did not realise her predicament.'

'Yes. Continue,' instructed the Colonel impatiently.

'So I crept up behind her ... and pulled it out.'

'Pulled it out? Suffering sergeants! You actually interfered with the woman's person?' The already excruciating pain in the Colonel's big toe got worse.

'As I've explained, I was only trying to help. She showed her appreciation by giving me a belt across the face.'

'Good for her. You had absolutely no right to interfere with the woman. Whatever next? However, more worryingly, according to this letter, you actually repeated the offence some ten minutes later.'

'The second incident occurred under somewhat different circumstances,' cringed Fraser, wishing for the first time in his life he had never set foot on a bowling green, never clapped eyes on a bowl with its intriguing aspects of bias or ever executed a crushing forehand drive. He just wanted to be at home with his darling wife in the comfort of his bed.

'Go ahead, Woodcock. We are all ears,' encouraged the Colonel.

'A couple of ends later, by which time we were all bathed in copious amounts of sweat, exactly the same thing happened again. Her skirt rode up the cleft of her buttocks, even more so this time. It looked as though she had taken in washing.'

'Taken in washing? What on earth is that supposed to mean?'

Tommy Simpkins struggled, amid bouts of uncontrollable laughter, to explain that the skirt in question had almost disappeared up the aforementioned cleft. His white popcorn hair moved about in waves with the bobbing of his head.

'When I want your interpretation, Simpkins, I'll ask for it.' The Colonel closed his eyes in dismay. It was beginning to get too much for him. 'But surely, Fraser, you had learned your lesson from the first episode?'

'Of course I had. I'm not stupid. It wasn't me, you see, it was our number three, the one and only Tommy Simpkins here. He had obviously noticed her predicament and, to my horror, before I could stop him, casual as you like, he strolled up behind her and pulled the offending skirt out.'

'You little snitch!' yelled Tommy Simpkins.

'Simpkins, will you grow up?' warned the Colonel. 'But, if that's the case, why didn't she smack him instead of you, Woodcock?'

'I knew she didn't like having it pulled out, and I knew there would be hell to pay. So I crept up behind her and pushed it back in. That's when she hit me again, only this time she had her leatherbound scorecard in her hand.'

Stunned silence fell on the room; it froze in the atmosphere. From privileged positions high on the walls, past presidents closed their eyes in shame.

As punishment for his misdemeanours, a seven day ban from the club was issued against Fraser Woodcock. He was also ordered at his own expense, and as soon as possible, to despatch a large bunch of flowers to the offended party with sincere apologies from both him and the club.

Upon his return home, Fraser discovered his wife in bed with yet another of her male friends. He heard the voice of Jimmy Young drifting from her radio as he gently pushed open the bedroom door.

'Had a good morning, dear?'

'Sssh!' she replied. 'Jimmy and this lawyer chappie are discussing the problem of modern day sexual harassment. It's very interesting.'

'Oh,' said Fraser, almost running out of the room. I think I'd better put the kettle on.'

6

What's in a Name?

When Stella Dodds arrived at the clubhouse two or three of the ladies were already clustered around the notice board, chattering away as usual in laughing, friendly voices.

'Where's Fitzwilliam Park when it's at home?' asked Gloria Bond, stretching on tiptoes to her full five feet and raising her glasses so she could read the fixture list.

'It can't be in the county. I've played on every ground in the county,' boasted Mary Pooter, towering above her friend and tracing a bony finger across the board. 'I never forget a ground, good or bad. Fitzwilliam Park – now that's a new one on me.'

Stella Dodd's ears pricked up. She knew a Fitzwilliam Park, a long time ago maybe, but she knew it all right. 'If it's the one I know, it's just over the county line in Coombe Rise.'

'That's it, that's the one. It says on their notepaper. Fitzwilliam Park bowls club are celebrating their centenary and have invited our club to send a mixed rinks team for a friendly game. Refreshment by way of a cold meat salad to be provided.'

Names were hurriedly scribbled on the team sheet. 'Shall we put your name down, Stella?' asked Gloria. 'You don't want to be turning down a free tea.'

Stella felt a strange lump in her throat as memories came flooding back. She had been born and bred in Coombe rise; fifty-six years ago to be precise. And Fitzwilliam Park

91

itself ... no wonder her mouth felt dry and a fluttering came into her heart. That's where she first fell in love, and you always remember your first love – or so they say. The first time is supposed to be etched into your heart for ever, and for a brief moment she couldn't even remember his name. Slowly the mists of time evaporated and a face and name appeared, as if from an old film. A dark-haired young man of eighteen, almost two years older than her. A tall gangling youth with an irresistible grin. Harry Hogbin, or 'Piggy' as she affectionately nicknamed him. She recalled the shock of wavy hair and the sallow skin. He claimed he was of Italian stock with a great grandfather somewhere back in Turin. That's where 'Hogbin' came from; it wasn't English at all.

Then she remembered how he had laughed and teased her about her name – Stella Barmie she was then. Whenever he called her on the phone, 'Are you Barmie?' was his favourite greeting. What a funny pair they had been: Hogbin and Barmie.

Stella allowed her name to be added to the fixture list. You never knew, she might bump into him, but inwardly she realised it would be a chance in a million. Still, she had nothing better to do. What on earth would he look like now? She imagined he would be married, with children and grandchildren, living in some far away country like Australia or Canada – certainly somewhere a lot more glamorous and exciting than Coombe Rise.

As she busied herself in the green stewards' office, counting the float and checking the rink reservations, she couldn't help the trickle of warm and happy memories that gradually grew into a pleasant flood. Both her parents were keen bowlers at Fitzwilliam Park. Her mother was the social secretary for the ladies' section, and her father good enough to be picked for county matches. She remembered helping mother, always a busy woman, and accompanying her to the local 'Cash and Carry' to buy such items as tea, coffee and biscuits for the match teas. They would scour the local stores to make up prizes for the raffles – bottles of cheap wine and boxes of chocolates with foreign-sounding names.

On occasions, when an important match was taking place, all able-bodied members were pressed into playing. Then Stella would help out in the green stewards' office as she was doing now. In those days the tickets were pulled off funny wooden rollers. One pound for a two hour session or two pounds for a full morning or afternoon session. Teas and cold lemonade would be served to the general public to help bolster club funds.

At that young age she never aspired to playing bowls

herself and her parents certainly never press-ganged her into helping out at the club. She did have an ulterior motive though: it enabled her innocently to bump into young Harry Hogbin.

Mr Hogbin senior was club captain at that time. A loud, brash man, who also teased her mercilessly about being Barmie, he never seemed satisfied until he had made her blush.

Unfortunately, his wife, Mary, was confined to a wheelchair and it fell to young Harry to accompany his mother at weekends to watch her husband play and enjoy the other outdoor delights of Fitzwilliam Park.

At times Mary Hogbin felt she needed a break from the slow pace of the bowls and Harry, with Stella, would take it in turns to push the wheelchair to whichever part of the park she wished to visit. The rose gardens were a particular favourite, where the fragrances drifted up into your nostrils. She adored the rich red flowers of 'Alec's Red', with its glossy green foliage, or the cerise pink of a 'Wendy Cussons'. Feeding the ducks and swans on the boating lake was another favourite. Together they would propel his mother up the steeper inclines while Harry, in devilment, would pretend to lose control as the wheelchair gradually picked up speed on the downward slopes. It was wonderful to hear a woman captured in a crippled body scream and shout in a magical mixture of fear and excitement. Always the final stop on their return to the clubhouse had to be the little wooden kiosk that sold ice-cream and brightly coloured ice-lollipops. They clubbed together what was left of their money to treat her, and always laughed as, week by week, she ate her way through the whole list of goodies. She had to try each and every one.

During the tea intervals the pair of them would scrounge enough money to hire a rowing boat. Most of the time Harry would row, his growing muscles propelling them effortlessly across the lake. Sometimes they sat side by side and rowed gently together in perfect harmony. Occasionally, Harry would allow her the privilege of rowing while he rested and laughed helplessly as they drifted around in circles. She remembered they always laughed at the same things and Harry saying she had an all-or-nothing face: either a straight, almost serious, expression, or a big, beaming smile. She couldn't do in-between faces.

When the skies were clear and blue and the weather really warm they would moor the boat and explore the little island in the middle of the lake. They would feed the swans and ducks and watch fascinated as the grey squirrels darted from tree to tree. They gave the secluded island silly names like 'Barmie's breakwater', or 'Hogbin's hideaway'. They had dreams of getting married and building a house on the island, away from the hustle and bustle of the town.

When the summer season finished Harry moved away to study at university. They talked endlessly on the phone and he would take her to the pictures or dancing on his free weekends. She remembered their first meaningful kisses, so full of love and innocence.

Then her father's firm of accountants had moved their head offices to London and he and the family had followed. Gradually, the phone calls and the letters petered out. She remembered taking his treasured photograph out of her purse as other boyfriends came along. They wouldn't understand the cherished memories of a first love; they would only be jealous.

The game at Fitzwilliam Park called for six mixed rinks, each consisting of two women and two men; another case of all hands to the pump. She was glad to see her name pencilled in at lead. All she had to do was roll the jack in the right spot, get her woods reasonably close and her job would be done. She could let her mind wander and exchange pleasantries with the other players on the rink. Charlie Simms playing at number two would be hard work though; he was as deaf as a post and she always felt uncomfortable when raising her voice. Madge Rollings at number three would liven things up. A bit of a character, she would insist on her opponents measuring every shot, and make sure players were behind the mat. The skip would be instructed exactly what he had to do, whether he asked or not, and be cursed out of earshot if he failed to deliver. But Madge had a heart of gold and could always be relied upon to be the centre of conversation at the tea break, declaring how she could never play on the same rink as her husband because they fought like cat and dog.

Doug Pointer, a crusty old bachelor, had been appointed their skip. He didn't believe in the niceties of calling players by their names; you were numbers to this retired ex-army drill sergeant. The expression on his face never changed, whether you played a blinding shot or a load of old rubbish. All things considered, Stella was more than looking forward to the day. She could take in the atmosphere of the park and relive the happy memories ... and she might just bump into Piggy Hogbin.

On the drive over to Coombe Rise, Stella sat next to Elaine Biddings, her usual coach partner. Two years younger, she still carried a full head of blonde hair, which put her own salt-and-pepper locks to shame. She had to admit it was now considerably more salt than pepper. Elaine's husband didn't play bowls. In fact, she was a golf widow and had only taken up bowls because her husband declared her to be absolutely useless at golf. The two women often took afternoon tea together and enjoyed many happy hours doing the shops. From time to time, Elaine had discreetly attempted to match Stella up with someone suitable, but nothing ever seemed to work out. Likely candidates were passed off as 'too short', 'too fat', or 'too old', nothing to get her heart jumping. Maybe she herself was getting too old or perhaps two failed marriages had knocked the stuffing out of any romantic notions she may still have harboured.

Her first marriage to a handsome thespian who thought far too much of himself, for all the bit parts he managed to achieve, lasted five years. Too trusting by nature, she had caught him with just one too many aspiring young actresses. After two or three trial separations they settled for an amicable divorce. As fate would have it, six months later he won a leading role in a sci-fi blockbuster and became a minor household name.

The second attempt at marriage turned out to be a little more messy. For the first couple of years everything in the garden looked rosy. Wedded to a high-flying financier, she enjoyed the luxury of a five bedroomed house in the country and a holiday apartment in southern Spain. Becoming over confident, however, he took too many risks and the business crumbled. To prop himself up he turned to drink, which only accelerated the spectacular collapse of his company. When he died she thought herself lucky to come out with enough money to buy a two bedroomed cottage on the outskirts of a small village. Nothing fancy, it boasted a decent-sized garden which, over the years, she had turned from a haven of weeds into a pleasant hideaway for her and her sole companion, Betsy, a cocker spaniel she rescued from a distressed animal centre. She supported herself by working as a full time secretary at the county hospital. By forgoing her mid-morning and afternoon tea breaks, she was allowed to take an extended lunch hour, which conveniently permitted her to nip home to feed and exercise Betsy. Things, she thought, could have turned out a whole lot worse.

Two weeks later the coach dropped them at the gates of Fitzwilliam Park. With an hour to spare before the game started there was ample time for a leisurely stroll through the park to get the circulation back into their legs. To Stella it felt like travelling back into a dream world, the memories gradually slipping into place with every step taken. Her heart skipped wildly as the boating lake came into view. Sadly, the old wooden boats had been replaced by brightly coloured fibreglass canoes and pedalos. Excitedly, she described to the other ladies the happy times she had spent here as a teenager. But she didn't tell them that if a boy loved a girl he would row her to the island where they would share their dreams of a future together.

The park seemed somewhat smaller now, but such things usually do with time. After enjoying the beautiful fragrances of the rose garden they reached the clubhouse. Entering was like stepping back into a time warp. Although the then separate ladies' and men's club had now amalgamated, little else appeared to have changed. Red and white bunting, the club's colours, hung from the ceiling which helped brighten the place up, but the faded photographs of past club presidents were showing their age. Her eyes scanned the pictures of past teams celebrating past anniversaries. She looked around for a friendly familiar face, but found none. Why should she? Most of the people playing when she was a teenager would have passed on to that great bowling club in the sky. She found herself inadvertently studying the men's faces. One or two smiled and welcomed her to the club, but she didn't know what she was doing. If Harry Hogbin happened to be in the club house it would be a chance in a million. How many times had she told herself that? And even if he were, she would have no idea what he would look like. Just concentrate on enjoying the day, she told herself.

Elaine Biddings stood in front of the mirror, adjusted

her cravat and straightened her hat. 'Come on, Stella Dodds. Buck your ideas up, we'll be on the greens soon.' She peered at her reflection in the glass. 'Why we have to wear these silly hats is beyond me. I look like a traffic warden on Brighton sea front. Mind you, there's a few men here I wouldn't mind slapping a ticket on.'

'Elaine Biddings! And you a happily married woman.'

Stella tied the laces on her bowling shoes and gathered up her two woods. On her way out she could not resist having a look into the green stewards' office. The little wooden rollers which carried the tickets had been dispensed with, in their place a small electronic till on which green lights flashed. The man in the office looked at her with raised eyebrows.

'Can I help you, dear?'

'Well, no, not really. I didn't mean to be so rude. You see, I used to help out in this office many years ago.'

'Did you now?' replied the steward, scratching vigorously at his left ear, which she noticed was considerably larger than the right one. She felt hypnotised by this strange affliction and struggled to break the embarrassing silence.

'While your ear ... I'm sorry,' she spluttered. 'While you're here, do you happen to know of a Harold Hogbin?'

The green steward scratched at his ear again, then switched to the top of his head. 'Hogbin, you say, madam? No, I don't think so. It's only a small club, you see. Would know if we had somebody of that name. Funny old name, isn't it?'

'Yes,' said Stella. 'It's a funny old name.' She turned away feeling foolish for having asked.

'Hang on a minute, my dear. Of course I know a Hogbin. It's all coming back to me now. Thought I'd heard the name somewhere, just a bit slow on the uptake these days. Hang on a mo, while I come out. I'll take you to him.'

Stella felt faint. 'You mean he's here now?'

'Been here a long time, as I say. Just didn't make the connection.' He closed his little office and she followed him outside, her head swimming and her legs weak at the knees. They stopped in front of a wooden bench and were confronted by a large, black gentleman.

'Here he is.'

'Can't be,' gasped Stella under her breath. 'Harry wasn't of West Indian extraction – not the last time I saw him.'

'Could you just move up a piece, Lloyd.'

'Certainly, man.' Lloyd smiled back. 'Plenty of room for both me and the lovely lady. Are you going to introduce us?'

'No, Lloyd, just push up a piece.' The steward nodded to Stella. 'There he is.'

'Who?'

'Your Harold Hogbin.'

Stella couldn't decide if she had suddenly gone blind or missed the point of some bizarre practical joke.

'Look,' motioned the steward, tracing his finger along the back of the bench and picking out the delicately scrolled lettering.

IN MEMORY OF MARY AND WALTER HOGBIN
DONATED BY THEIR LOVING SON HAROLD
1963

Stella's knees gave way and she almost collapsed onto the bench. Lloyd took her hand to steady her.

'Looks like the lady has seen a ghost.'

'Is that the Harold Hogbin you were after?' asked the green steward.

'Yes,' replied Stella, gathering her senses. 'Thank you so much for your trouble.'

'No trouble, madam. Glad to be of service. Now I must be getting back.'

Stella's breathing slowly returned to normal as, gradually, she recovered her composure. She studied the inscription on the bench. Lloyd watched with questioning eyes.

'Somebody you know?'

'Yes. A long time ago, but it still comes as a shock when you were very close to them and realise they are not around any more.'

'According to this inscription, over forty years. That's a whole lotta long time lady, but it's important only to remember the good times. Don't do no good remembering the bad times.'

'True ... very true.' Stella let her mind drift. There had been lots of good times, very good times.

'Like me, lady. I lost my good woman five years ago, but I still talk to her every day in my heart. You know what I mean?'

They were interrupted by Elaine Biddings and what looked like a search party. 'Here she is. We wondered where you had got to. They are just going out onto the bowling greens.' They stood back as Lloyd uncurled himself from the bench and stood towering above them.

'Me and the good lady just making our acquaintances. Very brief but very nice.' His captivating smile immediately turned the ladies' legs to jelly.

'You're a sly one,' said Elaine, digging Stella playfully in the ribs. 'Where did you find him?'

'Well, he was just sort of sitting there.'

'And you thought you'd keep him all to yourself,' laughed one of the other ladies. 'We are going to have to keep an eye on you, Stella Dodds.'

The bell sounded and the two teams, decked out in their whites, gradually sorted themselves onto different rinks. Stella found herself on number five. She noticed the gnarled old rose bushes had been replaced by pink hydrangeas. Sturdy concrete posts and chain link fencing stood where once the dilapidated larch lap barrier had swayed about in the wind.

Stella played the opening ends of the game as if in a dream, then pulled herself together. After the pleasant preliminaries on her rink had been dispensed with she found her gaze drawn to the opposing male players. Nobody faintly resembled the dark-haired youth of forty years ago. How could they? Half the men were bald. She couldn't imagine Piggy Hogbin being bald; he had had such a magnificent head of hair. Most of the other players were white, or rapidly turning white. Only two had kept their dark hair. One was barely five foot tall and as skinny as a rake. The other had black skin and was called Lloyd. Her head dropped a little as she resigned herself to her own foolish fate. How long had she been repeating that it would be a chance in a million?

Well into the second half of the game, and more by chance than anything else, her attention became drawn to rink number one. A resounding burst of applause caused

most people to glance in that direction. She watched a
player casually rise up off his haunches and put his hand
up to acknowledge the applause. She must have missed
him on her initial sweeping search, although he did appear
to spend much of his time squatting down directing his
team towards the jack. At first she only had a back view,
then, annoyingly, a side view. Very energetic in his
instructions, he bobbed up and down like a yo-yo – most
irritating. He was certainly of the right build to be Piggy
Hogbin. She waited patiently until the time came to play
her woods. After setting up her rink with two close woods
she whispered to Bridget Rollings that she would be back
in a minute. Trying not to attract any attention she casually
strolled behind the other players to the first rink on the
green. The two skips at the far end were preparing to play
their shots. She scrutinised the opposing skip, her eyes
slowly widening. It could be … if anyone could be, it was
him. She watched, mesmerised, as he delivered his first
wood. Arching down the rink, it clattered into the pack of
bowls, scattering them in all directions. A Fitzwilliam Park
lady stepped forward to inspect the result.

'Oh, well played, Harry, well played. Two shots.'

The other park players applauded in unison. 'Well bowled,
Harry.'

Stella stood frozen to the spot. She could only watch as
Harry accepted the compliments with a big smile, then
turned his back on her to commiserate with his opposite
number. Carefully she stepped on to the rink, trying not
to intrude. She asked a team-mate if she could see the
scorecard.

'If you must,' replied the number two, 'but it doesn't
make very good reading. It's their skip doing all the damage.'

Stella took little notice of the score; that was the last
thing on her mind. Slowly her nervous fingers ran down
the list of opposing names.

1. A. Mellish
2. R. Brown
3. F. Crombie
4. H. Beaumont (skip)

She blinked in dismay. There was no sign of a Hogbin. She *had* to make sure.

'Who's your skip?' she quietly enquired of the opposing team.

'Harry. Harry Beaumont,' came the reply.

'You're sure?'

'Of course we are. You count yourself lucky if you're picked to play on his rink – one of the best players in the county.'

Elaine Biddings stepped over from the adjoining rink. 'What are you doing over here, Stella Dodds? You're supposed to be playing on rink five.'

'We think she's after our skip,' quipped one of the opposing players.

'Yes, take her away. We don't want her upsetting our Harry,' complained a second.

Elaine looked with some concern at her friend. 'What's got into you today? First we find you with that nice black gentleman, and now you're after an opposing skip. Whatever next?'

'Oh, don't be so silly,' stammered Stella, her face flushing. 'I just thought I recognised somebody, that's all.' As she returned somewhat dejectedly to her own rink, she failed to notice a certain 'H. Beaumont' take a long, lingering look in her direction.

Back on rink five, Stella's lack of concentration began to affect her game. She just couldn't stop her eyes from wandering over to rink number one. By mistake, she rolled the jack into the ditch after Doug Pointer had specifically asked for a short jack. At the crossover he said nothing, but the disgusted look on his face expressed all his feelings.

'Sorry about that, Doug. A little lapse in concentration,' she offered.

Doug replied by shaking his head and thrusting his hands deeper into his pockets. She made amends by playing well over the last few ends and at the finish they conceded their game by only two shots. Ultimately, Fitzwilliam Park won by ten shots, which made for a very close and pleasant game.

Inside the clubhouse six long tables had been arranged with eight chairs to each so that players could dine with their opponents on the rinks. Laid out along the centre of each table were large plates containing salads, sliced beef, ham and liver pate. Mounds of freshly buttered bread filled the spaces in between. Large pots of tea were being trundled around on a trolley and placed on each table. As the crescendo of conversation gradually rose, Stella was unaware of a certain gentleman, who favoured her periodically with penetrating glances from the safety of his number one table. Something had clearly disturbed him. He felt certain he knew the lady from somewhere. When she looked across at his table he averted his eyes. Silly really, because he felt if he could meet her eyes he might remember where. In desperation, he quietly asked the skip on number five table to compare score cards. He made polite comments on the scores but his interest really centred on the names.

1. S. Dodds
2. C. Sims
3. M. Rollings
4. D. Pointer (skip)

Definitely no names he recognised, but there was something strange. Something connected to the immediate surroundings. The atmosphere in this very room disturbed him.

The meal came to an end and the two captains stood

up to compliment each other on the performance and conduct of their respective teams. The tea ladies were thanked for their magnificent efforts and the winning rinks of both sides received small mementoes of the occasion. Harry Beaumont, ever the gentleman, ushered his team before him. Passing close to table five he couldn't help but look Stella Dodds full in the eyes. It was a searching look, which she returned. Harry gave a half smile but Stella could only manage to slide her tongue over dry, quivering lips. Her heart beat as never before and she grabbed hold of the table to keep her hands from shaking. All too soon the fleeting moment passed.

The charity raffle brought the very pleasant occasion to its conclusion, the home team being fortunate to win the first four prizes. Stella came up trumps for the fifth and final prize, a box of chocolates with a foreign-sounding name. A spontaneous burst of applause came from Stella's team-mates.

'Good old Stella! At last we've won something.'

'Well done, Stella.'

Stella broke into a big, beaming smile. Inwardly, she cursed that she couldn't do in-between faces. She remembered it was something that Piggy Hogbin had always teased her about. Slightly flustered by all the attention, she endured the congratulations gracefully.

'Something to share on our homeward journey?' grinned Elaine Biddings.

'Save me a chocolate caramel,' begged Bridget Rollings. 'You know they are my favourite. Don't do my fillings any good, but I just can't resist them.'

Suddenly, from behind she felt a hand placed lightly, almost apologetically, on her shoulder. Then she heard the words that would change the rest of her life for ever.

'Excuse me, are you Barmie?'

Stella turned slowly around and lifted her head to look

106

into the dark brown eyes of Harry Beaumont. 'I used to be, but I'm not any more.' Once more she couldn't stop her face breaking into that big, stupid grin. 'It is you, isn't it? Piggy Hogbin?'

'Well, it used to be, but not any more.' He took her in his arms and enveloped her in a firm but gentle embrace. 'I wasn't sure it was you. I've been in a quandary half the afternoon, ever since you trespassed onto my rink. It wasn't until you gave that big, beautiful smile that everything fell into place. Even with the atmosphere in the clubhouse I still couldn't make the connection.'

'It was over forty years ago. I'm surprised you still remembered me.'

'Remembered you? Every time I come into this clubhouse I think of you.'

'I'm flattered,' replied Stella, 'but then you always were a flatterer.'

'A sincere one, I hope?'

'Of course, but I'm still confused. When I looked down your scorecard I couldn't find any Hogbin. What's with the Beaumont?'

'It's a long story.' He guided her to the door. 'Shall we take a walk outside? It will be a little more private.' Stepping from the clubhouse he took her hand and her heart completed another somersault, for only then did she notice the wedding ring. Well, at least I've met him again, she thought. Why shouldn't he be married? He was a good enough catch for any woman.

'There's something I want to show you.' He stopped at the wooden bench she had sat on earlier.

'I've already seen it,' she confessed. 'When we first arrived I inquired of the green steward if Harry Hogbin was a member of this club. He brought me out here. He said this was the only Hogbin he knew. When I read the inscription I wanted to cry.'

'Oh, my dear Stella, it shouldn't upset you. I had it put there especially to remember the good times. You know how much my mother and father enjoyed this place.'

Stella dabbed tentatively at her eyes with a tissue. 'It upset me so much to find out about your parents. Looking back, I realised some of the happiest days of my life were spent here with you, Harry Hogbin or Beaumont, or whatever you call yourself. There's so much I want to know about you and so little time, the coach will be leaving soon.'

They sat down and Harry took both her hands in his. The memories of all those years ago engulfed the two of them warmly.

'Every time I've set foot in the clubhouse I've thought of you, my little Stella Barmie. I wondered what life had given you; if you were married, had children. You just have to tell me everything about you.'

'No, you first, Harry, please. I shall die if I don't know. I'm intrigued by the "Beaumont" name.

Harry stood up and pulled her to her feet. 'Come on, let's walk down by the lake. That will bring back a few memories.'

'Some of the happiest in my life,' she said, squeezing his arm. 'Come on. Tell me – quickly.'

'There's not much to tell, really. Funny how things never turn out the way you plan them. Where did we get up to?'

'You deserted me to go to college, remember?'

'Deserted? That's hardly being fair, my sweet. But you're right. I remember I was halfway through my studies when dad died suddenly from a heart attack. We always thought mother would go first, her being in a wheelchair and everything. Father's death came as a big shock, so I left college. I couldn't leave mother on her own. I was all she had left in the world. So I came back home to look after her. I worked a few hours in the evenings just to keep some money coming in. Mother died two years later. I think losing dad so suddenly knocked the stuffing out of her. She wanted me to get out and meet a nice girl, but she was the only girl for me at that time. Anyway, after she died I had the bench made and placed in that particular spot. It just seemed right at the time.

'After that I didn't go back to college. I never had the heart for it. I fell in love with a nurse who had helped me with mother, and her father gave me a job running his building firm. She insisted that no way would she turn into a Hogbin so, just to please her, when we married I changed my name to hers, Beaumont. You would have approved of Amanda – so much like you, full of the joys of life. Three years later, and before we could have children, she was struck down with multiple sclerosis. She also, God bless her, finished up in a wheelchair. The story of my life, I'm afraid.'

Without thinking, Stella took hold of Harry's hands and kissed them. 'Oh Harry, I'm so sorry. You deserve so much more.'

'Amanda died eight years ago now. It was a blessed relief for her and more heartache for me. I wear the wedding ring so I never forget her.' He smiled wanly.

A shout from the clubhouse informed them that the coach would leave in five minutes.

'Come on then, Mrs Dodds, is it? I'll walk you back to the coach. I still want to know all about you.'

'There's not much to know really,' said Stella, wondering where to begin. 'I've been married twice.'

'Twice? You have been busy.'

'Busy perhaps, but not very lucky. Two failed marriages is nothing to be proud of.' She felt almost ashamed.

'I always thought you would make a wonderful wife. Mother said so, many times.' He put a protective arm around her shoulders.

109

'The marriage breakdowns were nothing I couldn't cope with. I should have seen them coming. But I've got my own little cottage now and I'm still working. Things could be a lot worse – and now I've found you again.'

They stood together watching the people clamber aboard the coach.

'You're deserting *me* this time,' complained Harold, giving her a goodbye kiss. 'But not for long. I'll give you a ring as soon as you get home. Is that all right?'

'Piggy Hogbin, if you don't I shall be extremely annoyed. Just give me time to have a nice soak in the bath and settle down in my favourite armchair with a large gin and tonic. Then I want to hear you talking to me all night long.'

He kissed her gently once more. 'You really are Barmie,' he said.

7

A Contract With the Devil

Thelma Moon carried out her domestic tasks of dusting and polishing more as a therapeutic exercise than a chore. The only part she never enjoyed was the mantelpiece in the lounge. Placed upon it amongst other ornaments, like the pair of porcelain entwined cherubs and a miniature mosaic of a Greek urn, stood her pride and joy: a silver lattice-worked frame displaying a photograph of her one and only offspring, Ely. The picture had been taken some four years ago when he was eighteen and had just left the comfort and protection of her bosom. For three of those years he worked diligently at university, studying in his father's footsteps to become an engineer. Then, for no apparent reason he decided to take a year off and had disappeared into the mysterious sub-continent of India or some other part of Asia. The absence of information regarding his exact whereabouts preyed upon her mind, for in all the twelve long months no postcard, letter or message had been received. Unusual indeed, because throughout his young life Ely had never once forgotten her birthday. Tears welled up in her eyes and a lump came to her throat as she clutched the frame to her bosom and cleaned its glass on her pink angora jumper.

Horace Moon, an amiable man with flushed cheeks and receding white hair, poked his head around the door.

'I'm going down the garden to lift your potatoes. Is there

anything else you'll be wanting? There are still some cabbages and onions in prime condition.'

Thelma carefully replaced the picture frame on the mantelpiece and blinked away her tears. 'Yes, dear, a nice large onion will be fine; if not, two smaller ones. I'll do liver and onions with some mashed potatoes.'

'Sounds fine to me,' replied Horace.

Thelma sniffed away her tears and moved on to polish the nest of mahogany tables. 'It was one of his favourites, you know – liver and onions. Ely loved them.'

'Oh him,' said Horace, raising his eyebrows. 'I always thought sausage and mash were his favourite, although he did enjoy his liver and onions. To tell the truth he loved all your cooking, you spoiled him rotten. Fat lot of good it did you.'

No longer able to control her feelings Thelma collapsed into the comfort of an armchair, her ample bosom rising and falling in convulsions. 'Don't be like that, Horace. Do you think we will ever see him again? Oh, why didn't he have the gumption to stop on at college and finish his studies?'

Horace placed a comforting arm around his wife. 'Of course we'll see him again – whenever he gets whatever it is out of his system.'

'But not a word for over a year, not a single postcard. That's what I can't understand.'

Horace looked steadfastly out of his flat eyes. 'Well, you've got to realise that when you journey to these large countries, the deeper you travel into the hinterland the more difficult it becomes to get word out. It's a bit like the early missionaries. Sometimes years passed before anyone heard anything of them.' He deliberately avoided saying that sometimes the missionaries never came out at all.

Thelma pulled herself together, brushed down her skirt and carried on with her housework. 'I just hope he doesn't catch anything nasty like malaria or beri-beri, and that he's got a decent change of underwear with him.'

A short while later, and sweating from the exertions of his harvesting, Horace pushed open the kitchen door. He placed a basket containing potatoes and onions on the drainer, then with a flourish set a bundle of mud stained rags alongside them.

'What on earth is that disgusting object?' complained Thelma. 'You're making a mess all over my kitchen sink. Take it outside, for goodness' sake.'

'Hang on a minute,' replied Horace excitedly. 'I discovered it under the last potato I pulled out. Really deep it was. Had a bit of a struggle with it, I can tell you.' He removed his gardening gloves and tentatively unwrapped the filthy bundle. The last of the rags crumbled to pieces in his hands.

'Horace Moon!' exclaimed Thelma.

'Look! There's some sort of box.' Horace cleared a fresh place on the drainer and set the box down on last week's copy of *The News of the World*. Mildew and slime covered the rotting wood and age had sealed the lock with rust. He attempted to lever it open with a knife but received a slap on the wrist for his efforts.

'Not with that! It's my best knife. I carve the Sunday roast with that.'

Horace fiddled about in the drawer until he found a screwdriver. Carefully, he loosened the lid and stepped back as if half expecting a genie to materialise. A small puff of white smoke swirled into the air, crackling and glowing silver before disappearing.

'It's a bomb!' shrieked Thelma preparing to hurl the pan of cold water she had readied for the potatoes.

'No, it's not,' said Horace calmly, forcing himself closer and lifting out the contents with a pair of salad tongs. 'Look! It's only a piece of paper.'

He removed the parchment, yellow with age, and cautiously unfolded it on the newspaper.

What lay before them made the white hairs on the nape of Thelma's neck stand on end and Horace blink his eyes in amazement.

'THIS IS A CONTRACT WITH THE DEVIL'

Sinister images in the margins of the parchment depicted the devil, with horns and a tail, and various potions and philtres. The signature, long and sprawling, spelled out 'Beelzebub'. The contract explained in demonic wording the method of selling of one's soul in exchange for a single wish. Smaller lettering at the foot of the page stated the contract was non-negotiable.

Thelma peered cautiously over her husband's shoulder. 'I don't like it. A contract with old Nick. What's he going to want in return?'

'How do I know? I'm not his advocate, am I? But just think ... if you could be granted any wish in the world, what would it be?'

'I would have our Ely back, of course,' answered Thelma without hesitation. 'I wouldn't ask for anything too demanding, like a new bathroom or a facelift. That would be pushing things too far.'

'Is that all you want?' asked Horace with a hint of disappointment. 'What about me? Don't I get anything?'

'Don't *you* want our Ely back?'

'Of course I do, but do you think this Beelzebub chap would throw in a small favour for me on the side?'

Mrs Moon studied her husband's face with some concern. What could be more fulfilling than having Ely back in their midst? The family would be complete again; absolutely no need to be selfish. 'Well, what do you want?'

Horace stroked his chin for a while. 'Let's see. I suppose

he could have a go at sorting out my piles; they've been giving me some gyp of late.'

'Horace, this is no time for flippancy,' scolded Thelma.

'No. Well, how about if he fixed it for us to win the mixed pairs in the bowls competition? After all, we're already through to the semi-finals. I haven't won anything down the club for years. Talk about being depressed. Not too much to ask, is it?'

'Not really,' replied Thelma. 'Mind you, we've only reached the semi-finals because Nelly Gasket's leg turned septic and Mr Carruthers sat on his glasses. No, I suppose it's quite a reasonable request under the circumstances.'

The accompanying instructions were read through with a mixture of excitement and apprehension. After lunch they decided to drive into town to procure the necessary ingredients for conjuring up a meeting with the prince of darkness. They purchased sulphur from the chemist, and a large roll of black sticky-tape from the hardware store. Across the street in Bellamy's *art nouveau* shop they bought four large black candles and some overpriced incense. Mrs Bellamy commented in passing on the unusual purchases, but Mrs Moon offered little in return, claiming only that they were surprise gifts for a very special person.

They took their evening meal of liver, onions and mashed potatoes with the accompaniment of two glasses each of fortified wine instead of the usual one.

A black and white film on the television flickered in the encroaching darkness until the midnight hour approached. Hesitantly, they prepared their normally quiet and respectable lounge for an audience with Beelzebub. Together they pushed back the sofa and armchairs and rolled up the half-moon rug. Horace, with the help of his trusty tape measure and frequent attention to the diagram set out on the parchment, laid out the pentacles in black sticky-tape. These accomplished, he joined the tips of the pentacles with an inner and outer circle. Satisfied, he removed the two short strips stuck to his slippers and the longer strip adhering to his backside.

Finding nothing more suitable, Thelma tentatively emptied the sulphur and incense into spare breakfast dishes and carefully placed them at the points of the pentacles. They stood the black candles on dinner plates and positioned them as instructed in the four corners of the room. Checking that the red velvet curtains were fully drawn and offered no gaps for nosey neighbours to witness their descent into occult, they lit the candles and turned out the lights.

'It's a bit spooky,' commented Horace, scratching at his groin.

'Quiet!' replied Thelma. 'You mustn't disturb the aura. Now we must divest ourselves of all outer vestiges.'

'What does that mean?'

'Take your clothes off.'

'What, all of them?'

'Yes.' said Thelma stepping over the tape to turn the photo of Ely back to the wall. 'Quickly now, before the midnight chimes.

The eerie silence was broken only by the snapping of elastic as Thelma removed her final garment. They padded softly into the inner circle and held hands. Slowly, their hesitant voices began chanting the words set down on the parchment.

'Louder!' ordered Thelma. 'He might not be able to hear us.'

'Any louder and the neighbours certainly will, protested Horace.

They continued their perfunctory chanting until the grandfather clock chimed midnight. On the final stroke a cold draught swept through the room causing the candles to flicker and the curtains to ripple. A white mist swirled

from one end of the room to the other, then disappeared under the door as quickly as it came.

'Ooooher,' shivered Horace.

'Shh!' warned Thelma, seizing the situation, 'I think we have to make our wish now. I'll go first.' She closed her eyes and Horace used the opportunity to view his wife naked, something he had not seen in a long time, and discovered, much to his disappointment, that her left breast sagged considerably lower than her right one. 'I wish for our one and only son, Ely Clinton Moon, to be delivered safe and well to his family.' Thelma opened her eyes and gestured to Horace to proceed with his wish.

117

'And if it's not too much trouble could you make it possible that Thelma and Horace Moon win the forthcoming mixed bowls competition at the Lower Moat bowls club? Not by too many shots, like. Just enough to make it convincing. Thanking you in anticipation.'

To their surprise nothing untoward happened. No claps of thunder, no flashes of lightning. Beelzebub himself declined to put in a personal appearance. In fact, the whole episode felt like a damp squib. The only occurrence of note was when Horace lost his balance putting his socks on and broke one of the black candles.

'Trust you,' scolded Thelma. 'Those candles cost three pounds each and all you can do is smash one and try to set the place on fire. I just hope it doesn't bring us seven years' bad luck.'

Somewhat disappointed at the barren outcome, they snuffed out the remaining candles, tore up the black sticky-tape and replaced the furniture. Thelma busied herself in the kitchen fixing the bedtime drinks, while Horace followed his nightly routine of closing the windows and locking the doors. Suddenly, the phone rang, shattering the eerie silence. Horace took the call in the hallway. As he listened to the voice at the other end, his face turned deathly white and his hands trembled. The phone rattled as he replaced it on the receiver.

'Talk about a quick worker. That was none other than Sybil Trotter-Brown, apologising for disturbing us so late in the evening.'

'What on earth does she want at this time of night?' asked Thelma.

Horace swallowed hard and wiped his tongue over his lips. 'She phoned to explain that her husband...'

'So called husband!' corrected Thelma.

'Her husband has gone down unexpectedly with sickness and palpitations of the heart, and therefore they have to

118

concede the semi-finals of the mixed pairs. That means we're in the finals at the weekend, my little cherry pie.'

Over the ensuing couple of days nothing out of the ordinary occurred to reinforce the notion that the devil was indeed a fast worker. Although pleased for her husband, Mrs Moon did her best to conceal her own disappointment at the lack of news of her son Ely. Horace comforted her, taking great pains to point out it might take some time for Ely to return home from the India, or wherever he was. He just couldn't be materialised out of thin air. Thelma contented herself by laundering their bowling whites. She wanted them to look their best in the finals. Perhaps the local press would be covering the occasion.

After a light Sunday lunch, and no more development on the Beelzebub front, they drove across town to the bowls club. From a cloudless sky a warm sun shone on their faces giving them a keen sense of anticipation. If they had half expected to be the centre of attention with their rapid progress into the mixed pairs final, however, they were soon disappointed. All animated discussions in the clubhouse concerned the previous afternoon. Lower Moat bowls club, for the first time in its history, had been selected to host the county finals of the women's triples competition, an honour keenly contested by all clubs in the area.

Various club members recounted different stories of the local vagabond who lived like a wild man in the woods surrounding the clubhouse. He had chosen that very afternoon to stage one of his more bizarre performances. His screaming and wailing from the depths of the woods put some of the more fainthearted lady bowlers quite off their game. Throughout the competition he had jumped out at various intervals from behind the evergreen hedges and bushes that surrounded the rinks.

He leapt up and down screaming gibberish at the top of his voice. If the upsetting sound of his antics failed to put the ladies off, his appearance certainly did. Completely naked and covered from head to foot in mud and accumulated filth, he looked like the wild man of Borneo. From behind a mass of unkempt hair and wild, staring eyes he succeeded in scaring all the players off the greens and into the safety of the clubhouse. While they were discussing their predicament the wild man scooped up all the jacks and ran screaming back into the woods. The competition could only be restarted and subsequently concluded with the positioning of male members of the club at strategic stations around the greens.

Mr and Mrs Moon politely shook hands with the couple who were to provide the opposition in the mixed pairs final. In size and shape they presented a marked antithesis.

Mary Christmas turned out to be the most slight and dainty woman you could ever wish to meet. So slight one thought that the merest puff of wind would blow her away. The smallness extended to her voice, so tiny she sounded like a child. She wore her greying hair swept off her face in the most charming of French pleats. On the other hand, her husband, Arthur Christmas, was a huge man, well over six feet in height and almost the same in girth. He possessed a booming voice, which resonated as if emerging from the depths of a coal cellar. His most peculiar features, however, were his feet, which must have been size twelve if they were an inch. To extend their dramatic effect they protruded almost at right angles, causing him to shuffle along like an obese Charlie Chaplin.

'If that madman comes anywhere near these rinks this afternoon I'll have his guts for garters,' bellowed Arthur so loudly that Mrs Christmas admonished him with a wave of her tiny finger.

'Well, it shouldn't be allowed, frightening people like that. Should be rounded up and put in the loony bin,' continued Arthur, grumbling away to himself like a volcano.

'Quite right,' agreed Thelma Moon. 'It's bad for the reputation of the club, and as for the local inhabitants, they must be quite scared out of their wits.'

After changing into immaculate bowling attire the four contestants strode onto the bowling arena accompanied by polite applause. Mr and Mrs Moon carried their woods in matching blue and green monogrammed bags, while Arthur Christmas cradled his own woods in one massive arm with his wife's and the jack in the other. It was like comparing cannon balls to marbles. Heaven help the Moons if he decided to play a mainly firing game.

The contest proceeded at a leisurely if one sided pace until, after ten ends, the Christmases enjoyed a fifteen shots to nil advantage. Mrs Moon, rapidly losing patience with her husband's wayward bowling, ushered him out of earshot of their opponents when they crossed over after the tenth end.

Under the pretence of straightening his tie she uttered through clenched teeth: 'Horace, what would you say if I said you were bowling rubbish?'

Horace looked both bemused and hostile. 'You say it loud enough in front of all these people and I'll probably punch you on the nose.'

Thelma tossed her head angrily. 'I thought as much. What would you do if I just *thought* you were bowling rubbish?'

'That's different. I can't do anything about what you're thinking in your pretty little head, can I?'

'Good. Well, I think you're bowling absolute rubbish. Now buck your ideas up or it will be another three years before you win anything.'

'I can't understand,' mused Horace. 'I thought we had this contract with the devil. He's got a funny way of showing it.'

'If I were you I would give up on that notion. It was a

stupid idea from the start. We've got about as much chance of winning this game as seeing our Ely again. Now pull yourself together so that we can at least put a few points on the scoreboard and go out with a bit of dignity.'

On the following two ends they dropped another three shots. You could forgive the Christmases for thinking that Christmas had arrived early that year. Then, on the thirteenth end, a strange incident happened. Arthur stepped off the rink and up the bank to pick up his hat as the fierce rays of the sun were beginning to give him a headache. On collecting it, and being momentarily distracted by shouts of encouragement from nearby spectators, he lost his footing, slipped down the bank and rolled into the narrow ditch where he joined two of Horace Moon's overplayed woods. With both hands trapped behind him, the harder he struggled the more he sank into the ditch. Eventually, he became firmly wedged.

Mary Christmas drew her slender frame up to its full four-and-a-half feet and remonstrated with her husband to stop messing about and take up his position back on the rink. But Arthur was well and truly stuck, and, to make matters worse, both he and the air around him began to turn blue. The match umpire was called for. However, even with the help of three able bodied assistants he failed to dislodge the hapless Arthur who by now had started squealing like a pig. The head groundsman came running over and, after urgent discussions, opined that the best way out of the predicament would be to fetch the hosepipe, turn the water full on and attempt to float him out.

Once the hosepipe had been successfully reeled into position a further discussion took place and it was unanimously agreed that Bartholomew Grant would administer the water, owing to his long experience as a part time fireman. Bartholomew expertly played the water over the distraught body of Arthur Christmas, watched by an interested and appreciative audience.

After a few moments of this treatment, expert or otherwise. Arthur let forth another outburst of high pitched squealing. Mary Christmas decided she had witnessed enough of this folly. Suddenly possessed of a voice loud enough to be heard in the next county (it's surprising how desperate times can bring about a dramatic change in one's personality), she ordered the groundsman to turn the water off or his life wouldn't be worth living. Then she set about Bartholomew Grant, warning him that if he did not instantly drop the hosepipe nozzle he would have it shoved up somewhere so hard he wouldn't be able to sit down for a month.

'He could have drowned, you know,' grumbled Mary as she calmed down, her voice gradually rising several octaves until it regained its wonted pitch. 'He can't swim, you see. He's afraid of water – and those two idiots doing their best to drown him.' She knelt down by her husband and wiped the water off his face with her bowls towel. 'There, there, my little pussy cat, we'll soon have you out of this ditch,' she crooned, as Arthur opened and closed his mouth like a beached whale.

The groundsman now came up with a third plan of action. Since both Arthur and the ditch had received a good soaking and were consequently slippery, he organised two volunteers to take a foot each. On a count of three they pulled simultaneously whereupon two surprised men fell onto their posteriors in unison, each clutching a size twelve shoe. Arthur stayed put.

Following another hurried conversation between the groundsman, umpire and Mary Christmas, towels were wrapped around the ankles of the unfortunate Arthur. Four helpers pulled together upon instruction. They were immediately rewarded with a slurping sound and the sight of bubbles rising up between Arthur's legs. After a second, more sustained effort, the body actually moved forward an inch or two.

'He's coming! He's coming!' shouted the umpire, jumping up and down.

'Don't you dare hurt him,' warned Mary, chewing nervously on her towel.

With encouraging shouts from nearby onlookers the rescue team redoubled its efforts and was caught by surprise when the body suddenly popped out of the ditch like a cork out of a bottle. Once again the ill-fated rescue squad were unceremoniously dumped on their backsides to the accompaniment of mingled shouts of encouragement and ridicule from the spectators.

The limp body of Arthur Christmas was laid carefully on the grass and tenderly sponged down. The whole episode had left him too weak and exhausted to get to his knees so the groundsman sent for a stretcher. Much to the chagrin of Mary Christmas the umpire slowly counted up to ten over the incapable form of her husband, declared him in no fit state to continue and awarded the match and the mixed pairs championship to Mr and Mrs Moon.

The interest and congratulations offered to the new champions turned out to be short-lived. The spectators who had started to disperse now that the free entertainment had finished had their interest revived by another outburst of squealing. The stretcher bearers, struggling valiantly to carry the not insubstantial Arthur Christmas, were taken completely by surprise when, without warning, the stretcher split asunder depositing its patient down the bank at the other end of the green.

'Crikey! He's going to get stuck in the other ditch!' shouted one of them. They looked on in horror as Arthur rolled helplessly towards the ditch. Visions of the hosepipe being rapidly deployed for another flushing out swept through their minds.

Shouts of 'Look out! Look out!' came too late as the revolving body collided with Betty Caruthers and Mrs Delaney who were taking a break from their singles final. The surprised pair finished in the ditch with Arthur briefly on top of them before he rolled away onto the green. Mrs Delaney, being of mixed Irish and Scottish blood, possessed a very short temper.

'What on earth do you think you are doing? You stupid, stupid man!' she lashed out at a defenceless Arthur. 'We are in the middle of a final here! Have you no respect, you big oaf!'

Mary Christmas witnessing the plight of her beloved, raced across the greens like a scalded cat.

'Don't you dare touch my Arthur, you spiteful old bitch!' she screamed and immediately set about Mrs Delaney, knocking her hat off and pulling spitefully at clumps of blue rinsed hair. Poor old Betty Caruthers lay stunned and bemused by the whole situation. It fell to the match umpire to muster the decency and haste to pull her skirt and petticoat back from over her head to a more respectable level. Pandemonium reigned until the two fighting 'hell cats' were separated and restrained at opposite ends of the greens.

Just as the afternoon appeared to be settling down and the luxury of calm restored at last, more high pitched shrieking erupted, this time from the bushes and greenery surrounding the bowling rinks. The 'wild man of Borneo' decided to put in a Saturday afternoon personal appearance. Naked from head to foot and filthy as muck in a bucket, he darted backwards and forwards, taunting players and spectators alike. Several of the braver and more agile bowlers closed in and cornered him against the rear of the clubhouse.

'Turn the hose on him!' shouted one of the members. 'That should teach him a lesson. At least he'll get a good wash.'

Thelma Moon who was closest to the hosepipe, instinctively picked it up, and, much to Bartholomew Grant's dismay, because he was too slow to catch a cold, began hosing the wild man down. She managed the jet of water expertly, up and across, and even succeeded in spinning her victim around in circles. Amid much screaming and protestation the muck and filth that had built up over the months started to wash off. A lily-white skin began to emerge through the streaks of mud. Spurred on by her success Thelma aimed the jet of water towards the head. Gradually the mud-caked dreadlocks disintegrated to reveal long black hair, and certain features of his face became visible. For a brief moment she diverted the jet of water and looked incredulously at these features. Unable to believe her eyes, she gave the startled face a thorough rinsing. Then she stopped, and moved a step closer.

'Is that you, Ely? Is that you, Ely Clinton Moon?'

The wild man ceased his infernal shrieking and covered himself as best he could. He blinked water out of his wild staring eyes.

'Is that you, mother?' he whimpered.

Mrs Moon collapsed in a heap on the ground. It was quite an afternoon for people collapsing. Horace hurried over to attend his wife.

'What's the matter dear? You look as if you've seen a ghost.'

Thelma waved a feeble hand in front of her. 'Look, Horace. It's our Ely, returned to the bosom of his family, just as we wished.'

'Bloody Nora! Would you believe it? We didn't wish for anything like this. It's just not good enough. I'll be having a few words with the devil when I see him. He's shown no consideration for anybody's feelings. And as for you, Ely Clinton Moon, just wait till we get you back home. You've got some explaining to do.'

That Saturday evening was a memorable one in the Moon household. After receiving two scalding baths and his first hot meal in months Ely was packed off to bed in a pair of his father's pyjamas. His explanation for such disturbing behaviour left much to the imagination. Apparently, his planned journey to the Indian continent had never got further than his home county. He had fallen in with a bad lot, lost all his money and become too embarrassed to ask for help. Instead of finding his true inner self and the meaning of life he had lost the plot completely.

Thelma and Horace discussed the situation until late in the night. At midnight precisely the phone rang. They looked at each other with foreboding. Horace placed the remains of his cheese and biscuits on the bedside table and picked up the phone. Mrs Moon slid under the duvet.

127

'Horace Moon speaking.' He covered the mouthpiece with his free hand and mouthed to Thelma. 'It's him.'

'And a good evening to you, Mr Beelzebub. No, since you're asking, we have not had a good day. In fact, we've had a very traumatic day. Got everything we wished for? Yes, but not in the way we expected. Actually, we've never been so embarrassed in all our lives. Right! As you say, our son has been returned to the bosom of his family, but we hadn't bargained for him to be returned as a gibbering wreck. Yes, it *is* the service I'm complaining about. Hardly first class delivery, was it? Yes, I admit we are the new mixed pairs champions, but it is the manner in which we accomplished it that we don't like. If I may be so bold as to point out, your presentation and customer care certainly need working on, Mr Beelzebub. My request, if I recall correctly was to win by a few shots, just to make it convincing. You couldn't even plan for us to win a single shot; we only won by default! It was the best you could do under the circumstances? What do you mean I couldn't bowl my way out of a paper bag? Well, now you are just being facetious. No, I'm sorry, if that's the best you can do it just isn't good enough. Given the chance I'd take our case to the office of fair trading, but it's hardly a viable proposition, is it?'

Thelma, growing more concerned about the situation by the minute, whispered to her husband, 'Don't upset him, Horace. He'll only get all riled up.'

Horace waved her away. 'Going to keep our part of the bargain? You must be joking. Yes, as a matter of fact I did read the small print. Yes, the clause stating the contract is non-negotiable. Well, what are you going to do? Sue us? I'll see you in hell first...'

Thelma buried her face in her hands and slid back under the bedclothes.

'And don't you threaten me!'

128

For Thelma Moon sleep could only be snatched in small, fitful bursts. Horace slept the sleep of the innocent, his snoring only helping to punctuate Thelma's troubled thoughts.

Refreshed from his night's rest Horace entered the kitchen, only to find his wife seated at the table holding a handkerchief to her red rimmed eyes.

'I suppose you're satisfied now, are you?' she sobbed.

'How do you mean?' replied Horace, glancing around and noticing an absence of any breakfast preparations.

'He's gone.'

'Who's gone?'

'Our Ely. Gone like a thief in the night, disappeared without trace. I told you not to upset that Beelzebub chap. Now we will never see him again. I just know it in my bones.'

'Of course we will, my dear. No need to fret. He'll come back when he's good and ready.'

The phone rang. Thelma jumped up.

'Don't you even think about it. You've done enough damage already. "See you in hell first" he says.'

Thelma took the call in the lounge, closing the door behind her. Horace strained to hear the conversation but all he could detect was Thelma's muffled voice rising and falling. She returned to the kitchen, a stony look on her face.

'You've done it now,' she said accusingly.

'Done what?'

'That was Mary Christmas on the phone congratulating us on being the new champions – amongst other things.'

'Poor woman. I suppose she's a bit upset, what with her husband and everything. Still, nice of her to offer her congratulations.'

'She's not half as upset as you're going to be.'

'How do you mean?' asked Horace.

129

'Well, where do you think you're going to collect your stupid trophy?'

'At the clubhouse, of course. They usually have a bit of a "do" on presentation night.'

'You haven't heard, then?'

'Heard what, woman? Stop talking in riddles.'

'Your beloved clubhouse was struck by a thunderbolt shortly after midnight. It's been burnt to the ground.'

8

Roll Up! Roll Up! All the Fun of the Bowling Green!

For ten wonderful years I enjoyed a very happy marriage. Well, as happy as any joining together in holy wedlock can be, I suppose. I think the main things that kept us together were – let me think now ... oh yes – the mortgage, and the kids of course. Then my husband, Russell – Russell Ball, to give him his full name – started to wander off the straight and narrow. Slowly at first, so as I didn't notice like; then, gradually, I cottoned on ... because I'm quick like that, see. My dad always said I was fast learner. Oh, hang on a minute. I've just seen my next door neighbour's sister arrive on her bike – must have a look.

Yes, as usual she's dressed in her full bowling gear. Can't say as I've seen her in anything else. White pleated skirt, them thick brown stockings – to cover up her various varicose veins, I suppose – and them flat brown shoes which I wouldn't be seen dead in. Today she's even wearing that funny hat which fits her like a boil on her bum; and, of course, her crowning glory – that navy blue bowls jacket covered in badges. She must be a really good bowler to win all them badges. As I say, I haven't seen her wearing anything else. I saw her a while ago in Tesco, doing her weekly. Then I saw her in the doctor's, collecting her prescriptions. Then I've seen her working in one of them charity shops – I think she only does one morning a week for the blind ... or is it the deaf? Can't remember which, and all the time she's wearing her bowling gear. Funny woman.

Now where was I? Oh yes, my Russell started going off the straight and narrow. He began by disappearing one or two days during the week, then it got to be all weekend. Never hardly saw him on a Saturday or Sunday. Eventually, I caught him red-handed. He brought this old bag home with him one weekend, when I should have taken our little girl to a birthday party which got cancelled at the last minute. I comes home early, see, and catches him in the kitchen with this old bag.

So I says to him, 'What you up to Russell?' And he looks at me all sheepish like, goes a bit red in the face and admits everything.

'This is my golf bag, Crystal,' ('cos that's my name, see). 'I've taken it up bit by bit so you wouldn't mind. These are my clubs. I haven't got the full set yet – saving up and buying them on the cheap. I was just giving the clubs a wash because I've got a competition tomorrow. Look! This is my driver, and this one is my putter, and this shiny one is my sand wedge.'

So we have a bit of a row like on account of him cleaning his clubs in the kitchen without my permission. Then we have a discussion about how we are spending all this time apart and how it can't carry on. The outcome of it all was that he had this wonderful idea that I should join his golf club – well, wonderful for him, like. So in order to save our marriage I took up golf. But it was quite clear from the start that me and golf did not hit it off, no pun intended. I spent a small fortune on buying all these golfing clothes, including a one-handed pair of golf gloves, which is of absolutely no use to anyone. I mean one hand is lovely and warm while the other one is freezing cold. What good is that? Then, for my fortieth birthday, Russell buys me a set of ten lessons with a golf professional. Dead romantic, eh? And there was me hoping for a romantic trip to Paris. I never knew these professionals swore so much. After my ten lessons they let me loose on the golf course itself. Bit disappointing really – I only managed the first three holes.

On the first hole I sliced my drive so badly it shot off at right angles and smashed the biggest window in the clubhouse. My second drive was even worse – it flew in the opposite direction and smacked the club president full in the mouth. Poor bloke, he was spitting blood and teeth for about ten minutes. He didn't speak to me after that. Come to think of it, he didn't speak to anyone for about three months.

The third hole finally convinced me and everyone in the club that golf just wasn't my game. In a desperate effort to keep my swing straight I missed the ball completely and hit the ground so hard it smashed the club and very nearly both my arms. The shock waves reverberated all the way up from my fingers to my shoulders and left my arms dangling uselessly at my sides for the best part of two weeks. I mean I walked around like a zombie. Russell had to dress me, and at meal times the kids took it in turn to spoon-feed me. When I eventually regained the use of my arms the first thing I managed to do unaided was open up a letter from the golf club politely informing me that my application for membership had been turned down. They added that, for a reduced fee, they were quite happy to accept me as a social member. Well, I wasn't feeling very sociable, see, so in spidery handwriting I sent them a return letter declining their invitation. The relief that spread across my Russell's face was a joy to watch, bless him.

Anyway, towards the end of last week I was chatting with

my neighbour, Mrs Belinkov. She's got a funny sounding name because she's married to a funny looking bloke from one of them Russian satellites – no, not the ones orbiting round the moon; you know, them satellite states – Belarus or Siberia or something . . . I can't remember which. Anyway, I was bemoaning the fact that I couldn't get on with golf, when out of the blue Mrs Belinkov suggested I take up bowls. She said her sister, Florence Earnshaw, was an avid bowler, and I had to stop for a moment because I thought she said 'rabid', as in mad like. Well, when I stop and think back she weren't all that far off.

I said, 'I've seen your sister. She's the one who always rides a bike wearing her bowling gear and that funny hat.' And she says, 'Yes, that's the one.' She told me that Florrie had lost her husband two years ago. Not lost as in 'died', but lost . . . and another woman found him and took him off her on account that she was out bowling all day and every day. But Florrie said it was good riddance because he was rubbish in bed and not very good at bowls – or was it the other way round? Anyway, next time Florence Earnshaw paid her sister a visit we were introduced.

'This is my neighbour, Florrie, Mrs Ball. You'll never guess what her first name is. Go on! Have a guess.'

'I haven't got time for guessing games. I've got to have my bunions seen to at twelve o'clock and then I'm playing in a match against a mixed President's team.'

'What! Real Presidents? Like Bush and Clinton?' I asked. Florence looked at her sister as though I were a few spanners short of a tool box.

'No, silly. Ex-Presidents of bowling clubs. Sorry what did you say your name was?'

'Crystal.'

'Well, I'll go to the foot of my stairs.'

Anyway, Florence made a big impression on me. I hadn't really seen a bowling outfit, not close up like. As well as

134

her navy blue blazer which had loads of badges down the lapels and a big one on her breast pocket, she wore this white pleated skirt which had to be a regulation two inches below the knees. Then, to set it all off, she had this lovely two-tone cravat which matched the band on her bowling hat, which I still say sticks out like a boil on your bum. But it was them horrible flat, brown shoes which put me off. I said, 'They don't really set the whole ensemble off, do they?' So she asks me what I thought she should wear, which was quite nice really because I don't know the first thing about bowls. When I suggests a nice pair of four inch white stilettos from Dolcis she looked at her sister as though I was completely off my rocker. Anyway, we had a laugh and she suggested that if I was interested we could meet down her club and have a roll up. When I tells her I didn't even smoke filter tips, never mind mangy roll-ups, she bursts out laughing fit to bust.

After she'd finished pumping up her bicycle tyres she told me that if I turned out to be any good she'd be looking for a new partner next season. Apparently, her resident partner had contracted Involuntary Rectal Prolapses, which meant that every time she bent down she broke wind and this was attracting some very unsavoury comments. Rumour had it that her membership would not be renewed at the end of the season and she definitely wouldn't be allowed to play indoors. Then Florence started making rude noises by putting the pump under her chin and pumping merrily away.

Two weeks later on a lovely sunny morning, the birds twittering away fit to burst, I turns up for my introductory roll up at Crappers Lock Bowls Club. Hardly an exciting or distinguished name for a bowls club, but beggars can't be choosers and I suppose I've got to start somewhere so I might as well start at the bottom – yuk, yuk. I wore my grey skirt, white blouse and a pink jacket, because I didn't possess a white one, and I wasn't going to spend good money on clothes like I did the golf and find out I don't like the game. I couldn't wear my flat golf shoes because they've got these dirty big spikes in the bottom. Anyway, I don't like wearing flat shoes because they make my feet ache, and then my legs start to ache to counteract my feet, and then my back aches to counteract my legs, and then I get one of my headaches worrying about it all.

I thought that, being as the grass was dry and cut ever so nice and short, I could play in my stocking feet, but the green steward says over his dead body. He asked me what size my feet were, which I thought a bit personal so I told him to mind his own business. Florence said I had to tell him or we would never get on the bowling green. So I whispered 'a size eight', and just to add further to my embarrassment he said he couldn't hear on account of his hearing aid being on the blink and could I speak up. So then everybody in the clubhouse got to know that I was at the front of the queue when feet were being dished out. Of course, Florence didn't help matters by saying she hadn't realised I had such big plates of meat and how my legs were far too skinny for such clodhoppers. Then she looks me all up and down, shakes her head and informs me that I'm completely out of proportion for a bowler. What with big feet, skinny legs, a big behind and a non-existent bust ... yes, completely out of shape to be any good as a bowler. Well, excuse me for living. It's the only body I've got. You can go off people, you know, and all of a sudden Mrs Florence-flipping-Earnshaw wasn't my favourite person.

Anyway the green steward started to give Florence a run for her money when he informed me that the largest size they had in the secondhand ladies' bowling shoe department was a size six and would I mind cross-dressing and using a size eight from the men's section. I could hardly say 'no', could I? Florence started fiddling with her handkerchief and getting all agitated, so I had to pay a pound to borrow a mangy pair of size eights which were in wide fitting, and I take a narrow; they had one lace missing and smelled to high heaven, which I objected to. All of this caused Florence to take the Lord's name in vain with one breath and ask him for strength in the next.

Then I had to have a hand inspection to find out what size balls I could handle. That starts me off laughing and Florence turns her nose up and says they're called bowls or woods, never balls. Then she starts on at my nails, saying that I will have to stop biting them or I will never come to much as a bowler if I don't possess any willpower or concentration. So I hands over another pound to borrow a set of woods that were covered in dust and hadn't seen daylight in years. Florence pointed out that the woods belonged to old Betsy Cunningham, who suffered from chronic arthritis in her fingers, which spread all over her body, until it reached her brain and killed her stone dead. I wish I'd brought my gloves with me. Then, believe it or not, they gave me a freebie. A tatty old string bag that had such a big hole it could only hold three woods – the fourth one kept falling out and rolling all over the place with me chasing after it and losing a shoe in the process.

I felt all inferior walking onto the greens because Florence was decked out in her bowling gear and pushing her bowls along in a neat little foldaway trolley while I had to keep bending down trying to round up my woods which seemed to have a life of their own. I think Florence would have liked to play on an end rink where I couldn't do much damage, but as they were all occupied we finished up on rink number four in between some rowdy gentlemen and six old dears who looked at me as though I was something the cat had dragged in.

Florence took her nice shiny woods out of the bag and made a big show of giving them another polish. Of course, I didn't have to take my woods out; they were already spread out over the grass on account of my bag having more holes than string. Florence smoothed her skirt, straightened her hat and leaned over to me.

'Whatever you do don't let your woods run onto the ladies' rink. You see that big brute of a woman, the one with legs like tree trunks and hands like Desperate Dan. That's Margery Bullock, the ladies' captain. Don't get on the wrong side of her or you'll regret it.'

When she came up to our end of the rink I could see what Florence meant. She was, indeed, a big woman. The back of her hands were ever so hairy and she wore them thick brown stockings you need a pneumatic drill to ladder. If I thought Florence had a lot of badges then Margery Bullock's jacket was like chain mail, and she had them down both arms as well.

138

'Morning, Margery,' said Florence. 'You're looking very fetching today, dear.'

You could have knocked me down with a feather. If that was 'fetching' I'd hate to see what ugly was.

'Morning, Mrs Earnshaw. I hope you're carrying out your share of the green stewards' duties this year. You were very lax about it last summer, if I recall.'

If she had been in our church choir she would definitely have had to stand with the men, probably in the bass section.

'Of course, Marg, I shall be doing all I can for the good of the club, now that I've packed in my part time job at the Chinese laundry,' replied Florence, rubbing in some hand cream that smelled like horse liniment.

'Good to hear it – and by the way it's Margery, not Marg. I'm not a tub of lard you know.'

You could have fooled me. She must have put her make-up on with a trowel, but it still didn't hide the fact that she had a moustache my Russell would have been proud of.

'Sorry, Margery. This is Mrs Ball – we're going to have a roll up. She's thinking of joining the club. You'll never guess what her first name is.'

'Hello,' I says, getting in first. 'I'm Crystal, as in Ball.' And she shakes my hand so hard I thought she'd nearly crushed all the bones!

'Pleased to meet you. I'm Margery Bullock, club captain. Be glad to have you on board. We could do with some new faces. Just a word of advice, my dear. Take that horrible jacket off if you know what's good for you – pink doesn't really suit you. Where did you get if from, a charity shop?'

Well, of all the cheek. Then she laughed like a horse and slapped me so hard on the back my fillings nearly fell out.'

'Only a joke, dear. I hope you've got a sense of humour.

You'll need one if you're going to play for this club. Crystal Ball indeed.'

So then Florence introduces me to bowls by showing me how to place the mat you have to stand on. And what a palaver she made out of that. Talk about being fussy. If she's as fussy as that at home it's a wonder she gets anything done. Anyway, she walks off up the other end of the rink and leaves me stood standing on my own. Then she shouts down for me to place the mat in front of the little number four. So I does as I'm told.

'No. Take it out of the ditch, Crystal. You can't play standing in the ditch, can you?'

So I mutters under my breath, 'Well, you're supposed to be the professional, I'm the learner. How would I know?'

'Put the mat in front of the number four on the grass about a yard from the ditch.'

Now I must admit I've never been much good with measurements, like, so I starts walking up the rink towards Florence when she shouts so loud it disturbs Marg the lard just as she is about to take aim with one of her woods. No actual words are spoken – this is a very lady-like game – but Marg just stands there glaring at Florence until she turns white and starts shaking, Florence that is, not Marg. Once she comes out of the trance Florence walks back down the rink and snatches the mat off me.

'I said a yard, not a backyard!' She looks at me as though I'm thick, then changes her mind and smiles ever so sweetly. 'Now I do hope we are going to get on, Crystal. If you could pay just a little more attention.' She takes a couple of strides from the edge of the rink and puts the mat down. 'I'm going up the other end again to stand in front of the number four. I'll give you instructions, then you can adjust the mat so that it lines up perfectly straight in front of the number four this end.'

When she reaches the far end she starts her nonsense again; I'm sure it was just a wind up.

'Step off the mat, please. Move it four inches to the left. Your left, not my left.' Well, she gets me so confused I can't tell my left from my right.

'Four inches' I said, not four feet! Now move it two inches back to the right. My right, please. Mrs Ball, you don't have to pick the mat up every time. Just leave it on the grass and move it left or right. Now you just need to bring the front of the mat round to square it up. No! Only about an inch. Put it back to where it was, now just pull the front a tiny little bit to the left. No! My left! Mrs Ball, just put the mat down and leave the damn thing alone!'

Of course that sets big Marg on the warpath again. 'Mrs Earnshaw! You should know by now we don't allow swearing of any description on the rinks. That will be one pound in the swear box when you get back to the clubhouse.'

I could sense Florence starting to get agitated again. She adjusted the mat some more – see what I mean about being fussy. She scooped up the little yellow ball and waves it about under my nose.

'This is a jack.'

'Why is it called a jack?' I asked in all innocence.

'I don't know why it's called a jack. A jack is a jack is a jack. That's all you need to know. Now listen carefully. I want you to stand on the mat and roll the jack up the other end as near as you can in line with the number four. I'll go up the other end and centre it up.'

'You're not leaving me again, are you, Florrie? I'm beginning to think you're making excuses just to get away from me.' Of course I said it tongue-in-cheek like, but I don't think Florence has much of a sense of humour because she started to blink a lot and grate her teeth. Anyway, I gives this jack thing a fair old whizz and it flies

141

down the rink, hits the bank and flies up over the railings. I think I may have overdone it, as Florence makes a big show of shaking her head, then storms off to try and find it. Unfortunately, she slipped on the bank and fell into the ditch. She had to hitch her skirt up to get out and I could see she were mad when she started dusting all the bits of grass off. I mean she looked so nice and neat when she started and now she's looking a bit dishevelled. Well, she recovers her composure, steps ever so carefully down the bank and places the jack back on the green. Then she stands there with her arms folded and asks me if it's in front of the number four.

'Of course it is, Florrie. I just threw it behind the number four and you had to go and fetch it.'

'No, what I mean is, is it *in line* with the number four?'

'Well, I think so.'

'What do you mean, you *think* so? You've got to be more accurate than that, and don't keep wandering off the mat. Now get back on the mat and tell me if the jack is in a straight line with the number four.'

When I'm on the mat I can see a mile away that it's not in line with the number four – I'm not a fool, you know – so I tells her.

'Well, which way do you want me to go?' she asks. Then she picks up the jack and starts acting all smart-arsed. 'Cooee, Crystal! Is there anyone at home? This is still a jack. It's not an incontinence pill or a suppository. Shall I move it so it's in line with the number four?'

'Yes, please.'

'Left or right?'

'Left.'

'Is that your left or my left?'

'I don't know.'

Then she sort of did a funny dance. 'Oh, for Christ's sake, woman, make up your bloody mind!'

142

Of course, that sets big Marg off again. She comes striding over.

'That will be another two pounds for the swear box, Florence Earnshaw. You're not setting a very good example to our new recruit. We don't want to lose her with your unnecessary shows of truculence. I suggest you try using a little more patience.'

'You need the patience of a saint with this one,' I heard Florence moan out of the side of her mouth. Snotty old cow. No wonder her husband left her. Imagine them trying to have sex. A little more to the left dear … no, not too much … shall we start again? – now right a bit … no, *my* right, not yours … up a bit … back a bit – what a carry on! Anyway, she said 'sorry' to the captain.

'It's your turn Margery,' said a faint voice from the next rink.

'Now don't you go rushing me, Mary O'Flaherty. I'll play when I'm good and ready. What are we? Still seven shots up?'

'No, I'm afraid we're three down.'

'Three down? Holy Mary! I can't leave you for a minute. We were at least half a dozen shots up when I left.'

'Mrs Adams got one of her lucky wicks.'

'Did she now? I'll have words with that Mrs Adams. She'll be on tea duties for a month if she doesn't watch her ways.'

Florence led me back to the mat, wiped her brow with her bowls duster and brushed at the last few blades of grass on her skirt. 'Now you do want to learn how to play bowls, don't you, Mrs Ball? You're not here under false pretences I hope. Because I'll tell you now, putting the mat down and placing the jack are the easy bits. The next stage might be a bit beyond you. Bowling is a very skilful game because your wood or bowl – never a ball, remember – will not travel in a straight line, however much you would like it to.'

143

'Why doesn't it go in a straight line then, Florrie?'

'Because it's got a built in bias, you see.'

'See where? I can't see anything.' I turned my wood over several times but blowed if I could see it.

'No, my dear, you can't see it. It's built inside the wood when it's made.'

'And this bias thingy, what does it actually do?' I was trying to sound interested, see, but to tell the truth I was more concerned about what I could get for dinner on the way home. Should I stop off at Leggy's the butchers and get some of them lamb chops that were on special offer, or would it be Sainsbury's steak and kidney pies which were in the buy-one-get-one-free deal.

'Well, what the bias does is when you roll your wood it will either go to the right or left. It won't go in a straight line. Have a go. Roll one of your woods up the green and see which way it goes.'

For once, I had to admit she were dead right. When I rolled one of my arthritic woods it all of sudden veered right and strayed onto the next rink where it gave one of the gentlemen bowlers a nasty crack on his ankle. It made him hop about and drop the can of beer he was drinking.

'Bloody hell, woman! What are you trying to do? Take the legs from underneath me?' He looked at the can, somewhat dismayed. 'There was still a good drink left in that can. Why don't you play on your own rink, woman? We were here first and we're playing on this one.'

Florence came to my rescue as she kicked the offending wood away.

'Serves you right, Billy Madison. You've been told before about drinking and smoking on the greens. I've a good mind to report you. Look at the cigarette ends and fag ash all over your rink. It's a disgrace.'

'You report all you want, Florrie Earnshaw. Just keep

that pal of yours away from my ankles or I'll report her for grievous bodily harm.'

'The only grievous bodily harm being done is with your smoking and drinking.' Florence brought my wood back for me. 'Take no notice of him, dear. It's people like him who give the game a bad name. Now where were we? Yes, well you see how your wood turned to the right? Now, on the other hand...'

'Oh, I don't think I could bowl left-handed, Florrie – not in a million years. Last time I did anything left-handed I caught my knickers on the back of the lavatory seat and thought I'd lost the use of my legs.'

'No, you see that's the beauty of the game. You don't have to bowl left-handed. All you do is turn the bowl around in your hand so the bias is on the opposite side. Go on – try it.'

She were dead right again. Halfway up the rink my wood decided it didn't want to be on its own, veered left and clattered into a big group of woods on Margery Bullock's rink. She started stamping her big feet so hard you could feel the ground move.

'No, no, no! she ranted. 'Don't say they've ruined the best end I've played all morning. We must have been holding eight or nine shots at least. Florence Earnshaw, I must please ask you to keep your friend's bowling under control. I think she's just robbed me of a full house.'

'Now don't get carried away, Margery. You were holding nothing of the sort,' said Mrs Adams, not in the least put off by her captain's ravings. 'We'll just have to call it a dead end.'

Florence simply stood there and glared at me, all rat-faced like. 'I told you not to let any of your woods go near her. You'll have to go and fetch it yourself. I'm not going.'

So I had to creep over to the other rink and get it myself. 'Can I have my ball back, please?'

145

Mrs Adams gave me a lovely big smile. 'Of course you can, dear. Don't worry, it happens to us all. Get her wood for her, Daphne.'

But Daphne was having nothing to do with it. 'I'm not touching it, she's playing with dead woman's woods. Look! See them initials: B.C. They don't stand for Before Christ. They belonged to old Betsy Cunningham — and we all know what happened to her.'

Funny thing, the way them ladies all stood aside. You'd think the wood carried the blooming plague or something. I looked at the initials — hadn't noticed them before — and there was an engraving of a skull.

'What actually happened to Betsy Cunningham?' I asked Florence.

'I told you. She got arthritis. Killed her in the end, but not before it drove her stark raving mad.'

'Charming! *Now* you tell me. The way them ladies avoided it you'd think she was a witch or something.'

'Well, if you believe all the stories about what she's supposed to have done to her husband, she could well have been. Makes my blood run cold just thinking about it.' Florence looked at her watch. 'Right now, time is pressing on and I think you've got the general idea of the game. I'm going to put the jack up. I'll make it a short one so that it's easier for you.'

So she rolls the jack up. I could tell it was a mile off line, but she didn't ask so I wasn't going to tell her.

'Now what we'll do, Crystal — we'll have to keep quiet about it of course — is we'll play for money, just to keep your mind focused on the game. Shall we say first one to eleven points for a pound?'

'A whole pound?' I said in mock amazement.

'Call it fifty pence if it's too much.'

'Hardly worth getting my purse out for a pound. Why not call it a fiver?'

146

'Five pounds? You sure?' I could see the cash signs lighting up in her eyes. 'I mean I don't want you to think I'm taking advantage of you. I'll go first then, show you how it's done.'

Yes, you go first, Florence. Don't bother about tossing a coin or anything fair like that. She made a big show about stepping onto the mat and giving her wood another polish. It finished about two yards short and a good yard wide.

'I thought the idea was to get it near the jack.' (Yuk, yuk.)

She looked at me as though I was something left in the toilet pan. 'First one's always a tester, dear, just to feel out the green. Off you go then. And make sure you keep one foot on the mat and check your bias before you bowl. Don't want to go upsetting Margery again.'

Well, I played my first wood. A bit too heavy I could tell as soon as I let go, but it followed her wood, knocked it out of the way and finished two inches from the jack.

'Beginner's luck,' she sneered. 'If my wood hadn't been there to stop it you would have finished up in the middle of next week. Now, if you don't mind, I'll just have to knock your wood off the jack.'

'Help yourself Florrie.' (Yuk, yuk.)

Her second wood finished more or less in the same place as her first. So I did exactly the same and knocked it out of the way, and my second wood finished up five inches from the jack.

'I wish you wouldn't keep banging into my woods, Crystal. They cost me a lot of money.' She bowls her third wood with a bit more determination; I could tell because the veins on her forehead stood out. I thought for a moment it would knock my wood out of the way, but it ran out of steam, pushed my second wood right up to the jack and then rolled away.

147

'Well, thank you, Florrie. Nice of you to give me some help. I know as I'm a complete novice I'm going to need it.' (Yuk, yuk.) I fetched the third wood and gave it a wipe with my handkerchief. I took ever so careful aim and – would you believe it – finished only a foot short of the jack.

'Look, Florrie. Just like they do on the telly.' I could feel right away she was a bit peeved.

'Actually a bit of a foul shot' she said, looking at my feet. 'You're supposed to have all your foot on the mat not half on half off. Though with the size of your feet I suppose that's asking the impossible. I'll let you off this time.' So, to show my appreciation, I does a funny little dance – you know, a bit like that moon walk stuff Michael Jackson does. She looks at me as though I've gone off my rocker. Anyway, it fascinated Billy Madison on the next rink and he tried to copy me, but he wasn't any good because his feet got all tangled up and he fell over.

Florence snatched up her last wood. 'Right, Mrs Ball. I want you to watch this closely.' Hello, I thought. Where had Crystal disappeared to? Getting a bit serious now, are we?

'This is what's called a firing shot. Get it spot on and I should knock all your woods out of the head.'

'What's a head, Florrie?'

'Anything that is in close proximity to the jack, of course!'

Of course! And *she* would know, not having one of her woods anywhere near the jack. (Yuk, yuk.) Well, she bends down, winds herself up like a spring and puts so much effort into the shot she nearly falls in a heap on the mat. I watch fascinated as her wood bounces along the green, turns sharp left and disappears up the skirt of that nice Mrs Adams on the next rink. I don't mean 'up' as 'in the air' like, but Mrs Adams happened to be kneeling down at the time measuring something with a tape measure. She gave such a jump and a squeal you'd have thought somebody had touched her up. (She should be so lucky.)

'Well, I never! Deary me! Where on earth did that come from? It's not one of ours.'

'I'll give you two guesses,' said Margery Bullock storming over to extricate the offending wood. 'And you can bet the first one will be Florence and the second Earnshaw. That's going to be teas all round when you get back in the clubhouse, Mrs Earnshaw. You've been bowling long enough now to sort out your bias.'

So I bowls my last wood, nice and gentle like, and it's good enough to finish only a yard from the jack. We walks up to inspect the head and, all of a sudden, Florence starts to limp.

'I think I've pulled a muscle,' she says, rubbing the back of her leg. 'I put far too much effort into that last shot.'

'What do we do now, Florrie?' (Yuk, yuk.)

'Count up how many woods you've got nearest to the jack.'

'All of them, Florrie?'

'Yes, all of them. All right, so it's four shots to you. Beginner's luck, I suppose.'

'That's four shots to nothing then, and the first one to reach eleven for five pounds?' (Yuk, yuk.)

'I do hope this gammy leg gets better,' she sighed. 'It's fair giving me some gyp. It's a pity I didn't bring my athlete's liniment with me.'

Then we starts all over again at the opposite end – and silly me thinking you only played at one end all the time. I managed to get the mat sorted out and roll the jack up; it only took about ten minutes this time so I must be getting the hang of it. The ice-cream kiosk is just over the back and there's a young mum sitting on a bench with a baby in the pram and it's bawling loud enough to get on anybody's nerves. She's also shouting at a young lad who's licking on the biggest ice-lolly I've ever seen. Poor Florence comes back down the green, limping when she remembers to. She's not looking too happy – nor would I if I had to pay three pounds in swear fines, and fork out for teas all round on account she put up a bowl on the wrong bias thingy. Well, I play my first wood and it goes rolling along and finishes a good two yards past the jack.

'Looks like your beginner's luck has deserted you already, Crystal. I didn't think it would last for long.'

Ooh, she can be ever so bitchy when she likes. Anyway, my second and third woods both finish well past the jack, just like my first one. Florrie's first three woods all finish up close to the jack and she's holding three shots, and all of a sudden her limp disappears and she's starting to show off a bit.

'Must be downhill this way, Florrie. You could have warned me.'

'Don't be silly, Crystal.'

I see we're back on first name terms again, on account of she's holding shot.

'You can't have an uphill and a downhill on a bowling green. That would be absurd. You just have to make adjustments for the wind. If you watch the flag on the clubhouse you'll notice the wind is blowing the opposite way – it's behind you now.'

Well, I plays my last shot, completely forgetting I've got the wind behind me, and it goes racing up the green between her woods, picks up the jack and takes it to my other woods at the back of the green.

'I don't believe it,' groaned Florence, 'How can anyone be so lucky!'

This puts her right off her last shot, so she turns round to the mother sitting on the bench and does a moody. 'Can't you keep that baby quiet? It's been screaming non-stop since we came down this end.'

The woman on the bench lifted up her rumpled jumper and pushed a breast into the baby's face. 'I can't help it, lady. I fink she's teething or somefink. She's getting on my pip as well as yours, you know, and I've got to take her home wiv me. I've only come to the park 'cos my Ron's on night shift and he gets all stroppy if he can't get his kip. You want to try living wiv a couple of screaming brats and a stroppy old man. Ain't no bowl of flipping cherries, I can tell you. Johnny, just you get your head out of them railings at once or the bowlers will have your guts for garters. You know what a touchy old lot they are.'

Little Johnny had finished slurping at his ice-lolly and was seeing how far he could push the stick up his nose. 'Hey, lady! What you got all them badges for? I fought you must be a good player wiv all them badges, but you ain't You're rubbish, you are.'

Well, that didn't please Florence one bit I can tell you, and her limp comes back again.

'I think I've got one of my migraines coming on, Mrs Ball. That baby's screaming goes right through you.'

'Is that another four shots to me then Florrie?' (Yuk, yuk.)

'I suppose so.'

'So that makes it eight shots to me and nothing to you?' (Yuk, yuk.)

'Yes. Well, get on with it I can't say I'm feeling in the best of condition, what with my leg and now my head.

Just as well she's past her hot flushes or she would be blaming them as well. So I puts the mat down, rolls the jack up and I was ever so lucky because it stopped about two inches from the edge of the green. Poor old Florence had to limp all the way back holding her head. I nearly felt sorry for her. Anyway, these long jacks seem to suit me, and I did really well because I only lost one of my

151

woods in the ditch while Florence lost two of hers and the other two finished miles short.

'Does that mean I've won then, Florrie? (Yuk, yuk.)

'It looks like it, doesn't it? I can't wait to get home and put my leg up.'

'What? You mean I've won eleven shots to nothing then?' (Yuk, yuk.)

'Yes, but please don't keep on about it. You're supposed to be magnanimous in victory. Of course, I didn't want to be to hard on you as you're a novice ... and what with my leg and now my migraine.'

'So I've won five pounds, and you being very nearly a professional. And you've got to put three pounds in the swear box and buy all them teas. Oh dear! Not really been your day, has it?' (Yuk, yuk.) I don't think Florence had any intentions of hanging about, as she gave her woods another polish, placed them carefully in her bag and strapped the bag on her little trolley. 'Hang on a minute, Florrie. Wait for me. I can't seem to keep all my woods in this soppy string bag. It's like trying to be a juggler in the circus ... Oh watch out, Florrie!' And there's Florrie hopping about like a good'un because a wood fell out of my bag and landed on her foot.

'You clumsy woman! Now you've crippled my other leg. Why don't you just drop a wood on my head and finish me off all together?'

'I'm ever so sorry, Florrie. Oh that's good – 'sorry, Florrie'. After you taking all this trouble to teach me how to play. Will you still be able to ride your bike?'

'Bike? If things get any worse I'l have to call an ambulance. Come on! Let's get going before big Marg spots me. Where is she, anyway?' And, of course, big Marg is standing right behind her.

'Going somewhere, Mrs Earnshaw?'

Poor Florence nearly has a fit and loses her trolley down

the ditch, and the little boy starts laughing which sets the baby off screaming again.

'Come on, girls. Time for a tea break. It always tastes so much nicer when somebody else is buying,' says Margery Bullock. Then she smiles at me and puts a big arm round my shoulder. 'And you, young lady, let me give you a hand with those woods. I'll have a word with Mrs Swinton. She's supposed to be in charge of maintenance. Yes you, young lady. We must get you a signing-on form straightaway. I've been watching you. A bit of training and experience and you could well turn out to be a county player in spite of that horrible pink jacket.'

Well, fancy that! Me a county player! You could have knocked me down with a string bag.

9

Daydreams and Chocolate

The two thugs stepped silently out of the darkness and pushed the startled young woman up against the wall. Her tumbling blonde hair framed a pretty but frightened face. Her jacket broke open to reveal a low cut evening gown and a diamond necklace shimmering on pale skin. She was indeed a beauty, trembling like a moth against the background of the dim street lights. The thugs licked their lips in anticipation; strong hands began to push and paw the soft, delicate skin.

'I wouldn't do that if I were you!' warned Vernon Spratt, springing out of the night like an avenging shadow.

'What! Where the hell did you come from?' growled the taller of the two thugs. His hair hung long, lank and black against a sallow face displaying an angry red scar from the side of his left eye to his chin.

'Yeah, where did you come from, shorty?' threatened his associate, shorter, and broader in stature but growing more in confidence as he realised the intruder was alone, 'Why don't you hand over your wallet and that fancy looking watch, and we'll promise not to cut you up too much.'

'If you want anything from me you're going to have to take it, and that's the last time I will tell you to unhand the lady.'

'And what if we just don't?' hissed the first villain, waving a switchblade inches from Vernon's face.

'Don't say I didn't warn you.' Vernon stepped back with the grace of a ballet dancer. The side of his hand flew under the blade and caught the thug firmly in the windpipe. Now they knew Vernon Spratt was an expert in unarmed combat – probably the most dangerous man in the world. The thug slumped down, gasping for air. He wouldn't be getting up. His companion, fear in his eyes lashed out with his blade. He never stood a chance. Vernon side-stepped his assailant and in one graceful movement brought his right foot up behind him to catch the thug full under the nose. Vernon heard the loud crack and knew his blow had been delivered perfectly. The man was out cold before he rolled into the gutter.

The young woman let out a faint cry of relief. Vernon grabbed her protectively and hailed a passing taxi. He gave the driver a fifty pound note and instructed him to make sure the woman got home safely. As the cab began to pull away she wound down the window and planted a kiss full on Vernon's lips.

'Thank you, my knight in shining armour. I'll never forget you.'

Vernon slowly awoke from his dream. The lingering kiss he could still feel on his lips had not, unfortunately, been that of the fair damsel in distress he had just rescued. Pinky, the Pekinese, had impatiently jumped up into his lap and begun, enthusiastically, licking his master's face. Gertrude Spratt watched critically as her husband gradually rejoined the world and, wiping his lips, pushed the dog away.

'It's no good pretending you're still asleep, Vernon. He knows it's time for his walkies. He should have been taken ages ago, and you daydreaming your life away. I don't know, Vernon, but these days you act more like a little boy than

156

a man of sixty-two. You haven't even started on your chores yet. Before you take Pinky out, can you get the shoe polish box from under the stairs? My bowling shoes could do with a good shine – and I suppose yours could too. We don't want to let our standards slip now do we?'

'No, dearest.'

'I would do it myself, but my back is so delicate these days I have to be so careful.' She selected a chocolate from the open box on the sideboard, one wrapped in red foil. She knew it off by heart: cerise – a whole cherry soaked in liquid crème kirsch and covered in delicious Belgian chocolate. 'I think I will have to take some of my pain killers to get me through the game this afternoon.'

'Please be careful with those tablets, dear. You do recall the doctor warning you that they are the strongest on the market, and should be taken only when absolutely necessary.'

'Just get the polish, will you, and do as you're told. I'm quite capable of looking after myself.' Her hand slipped back into the chocolate box as if attracted by a magnet. She selected a montagne, dark chocolate with a light chocolate mousse. Sheer heaven!

'Yes, dearest,' said Vernon, easing himself gently down onto his knees while Pinky jumped and snapped around his ankles. He pushed open the cupboard door and peered into the darkness.

'Are you there, your majesty?' he called in a reassuring voice.

'Yes, who is it?' came a frightened reply.

'It's Vernon Spratt, your Majesty. I'm in charge of the rescue team searching for you and other members of the Royal Family. It was actually Pinky who found you, although I have to admit I have trained him to absolute perfection.'

'I just knew it would be you, Vernon. If anybody could find me it had to be you. I just kept repeating it to myself; it's what kept me going. What on earth happened, Vernon?'

'Earthquake madam. I think the epicentre was practically the middle of Buckingham Palace. You're extremely lucky. There's only this part of the building that hasn't been completely flattened. Don't try to move. I'll endeavour to construct a makeshift stretcher.'

'Vernon, please don't leave me.'

'No intention of doing so, Ma'am. I'll just remove the arms from this Queen Anne chair, then I'll take you out on my back.'

'Have there been many casualties?'

'Hundreds Ma'am. I'm sorry to be the one to inform you, but I'm afraid the Duke bought it.'

'Oh dear! Poor old Dukie. Always in the wrong place at the wrong time. In that case, I'll have to make you my consort, Vernon. I don't know of anyone who deserves it more.'

With her majesty strapped safely to his back, Vernon, followed by Pinky, inched his way out of the rubble. They

broke through into daylight to the sound of cheering from crowds of worried onlookers held back by a cordon of police.

'There you are, your Majesty – your adoring public.'

'I think it's you they adore, Vernon. You've done so much for your Queen and country. Oh dear, Vernon! Just look at your blazer – it's torn to shreds.'

'Never mind, Ma'am. Pity it's my bowls club blazer as well. Never had time to change. When I got the message I rushed straight here.'

'Whom do you play for?'

'Gildrege Park, your Majesty.'

'For services rendered, above and beyond the call of duty, I declare it to be known from this day hence as *Royal* Gildrege Park.'

Vernon located the shoe box and backed his way out, banging his head and almost squashing Pinky in the process. The dog yelped, causing Mrs Spratt to come hurrying back into the room.

'What have you done to my poor little Pinky? You're so clumsy, Vernon. What took you so long? A simple little job like that. Day-dreaming again, I suppose. I think I'll make an appointment with Dr Brown, get him to give you the once over.'

'Yes, dear,' said Vernon. He never argued with his wife; in fact, he never argued with anyone. He was more than content at his time of life to trundle peacefully on. A short, thin man with a plain face and small eyes, so quiet most of the time he blended into the scenery like a chameleon. He dressed in plain nondescript clothes his wife always bought for him. He had worked as a bank clerk for over forty years – a solid, reliable worker, who only accepted promotion when it was thrust upon him. Were it not for the introduction of word processors, and later computers, he would still be working now. The change from pen to mouse did not suit or inspire him, so when his retirement came he accepted it with open arms. His cultured pen-craft was too slow for the hectic pace of modern times, although in his youth and early twenties his skill at calligraphy had won him many admirers and one or two prizes.

On his retirement he had taken up bowls, along with Mrs Spratt, in which recreation they enjoyed the gentle camaraderie on and off the greens. Here again Vernon Spratt preferred anonymity to the limelight. He rarely entered competitions, preferring to play for the club in friendly matches. He always played at number two, where he felt his only responsibility lay in keeping the scorecard. After the lead had played the jack and (he hoped) won the opening encounters, Vernon could then play his two woods to the best of his mediocre ability. Then he could concentrate on making his scorecard into a work of art. He never made any mistakes, only writing his numbers down when absolutely sure of the score. Once the numbers were entered in beautiful copperplate writing he would not change them; nothing was allowed to detract from his work of art. He made little small talk, even with his own team-mates, preferring to live in his own quiet world where he could conjure up enough adventures and excitement. Vernon Spratt, man of mystery.

Gertrude Spratt was the complete opposite of her husband. Whereas Vernon was small and timid, she was sturdily built and of an outgoing character. She enjoyed the spotlight whenever possible. Unfortunately, since her early thirties and with no sign of children, she fought an ever more hopeless battle with her weight. This she blamed on the lack of open love in her marriage. To provide comfort she turned to food, and in particular to chocolate, notably fine Belgian chocolate to which she had little or no resistance.

160

DAYDREAMS AND CHOCOLATE

The lack of demonstrative love in their marriage could be traced back to the early days. Both in their own ways were unprepared for the physical side, which had barely flickered, let alone burst into flames of passion. Vernon appeared quite content with a motherly figure, while Gertrude's weight and lack of physical beauty made her feel insecure and unworthy of love. She was more than thankful for someone to provide succour for her modest needs. Vernon could be relied upon to present her with his wages and a box of the finest Belgian chocolates every week.

Since retirement their life together more or less revolved around the game of bowls. For Gertrude this was a sport she could manage, even with her weight, and she lacked no skill in the finer points of the game. Unlike Vernon, she entered as many competitions as possible and her trophy cabinet displayed the rewards of her many triumphs. She admitted Vernon played his part in her success. As she didn't drive, he was always on hand to act as an accommodating chauffeur, ferrying her around to various tournaments.

Gertrude always 'skipped', even in mixed rinks. If she couldn't skip, then she didn't play – it was as simple as that. Captains who strayed from this when selecting teams did so at their own peril. For one thing, her loud, authoritative voice commanded respect. For another, if she had to get down to measure shots she would probably be unable to get back up again. In skipping she would not have a crowd of players behind, quietly commenting on her size. Yes, she had heard remarks behind her back, but nobody had yet dared to say them to her face.

Away from bowls, and if the weather permitted, she liked nothing better than to relax on the wooden bench in their garden. Here she felt comfortable, surrounded by brick pillars and six foot high peep-proof fencing. Pinky lay at her feet, one eye open for any trespassing cats, and the other on his mistress in case she felt in a benevolent mood and allow him the luxury of sampling some of the chocolates in the box by her side. Her hand reached out and selected another of her favourites, a marquise – milk chocolate praline, decorated with half a walnut.

Gertrude enjoyed this tranquil seclusion. At one stage they had worked side by side in the garden, tending the beds, pruning the bushes or cutting the grass. Alas now, owing to her ever increasing weight and consequent bad back, she could only manage the lightest of tasks. She closed her eyes and felt the warmth of the sun on her face. She fumbled into the box for another delight. This time she recognised it just by its flavour – a white chocolate one, this the pirouette – praline and crunchy biscuit pieces covered in sensual white Belgian chocolate. With the sun on her face and the chocolate melting in her mouth she dreamed of what might have been. Perhaps, if she had not been quite so plain, she would have attracted more lovers – dashing, exciting beaus who would have taken her dancing, or rushed her off to exciting places swearing their undying love for her. But these fantasies belonged only in the late night films she watched on television, or in the pages of her Mills and Boon collection. She unwrapped the foil from a gianduja, a smooth hazelnut praline covered in milk chocolate. She bit through the soft layers and passed half of it down to Pinky, who rewarded her by licking her fingers zealously.

Vernon could be heard at the side of the house putting their bowls into the boot of the car. They were playing at different destinations this afternoon. He would drop Gertrude off at Old Park. Today not only would she be skipping but acting as stand-in captain as Lily Coleman, the club vice-captain, had earlier in the week departed to St. Lucia for three weeks' honeymoon with her third husband. Some five years younger than Gertrude, she still possessed the gracious good looks that turned the heads of male bowlers. Gertrude had initially been jealous of a woman who had discovered a new and exciting love, but then realised she couldn't really be doing with all that. She had grown accustomed to the simple, reliable things in her life.

'The bags are in the boot, dear. I'm ready when you are.'

'You did remember to give my woods a good polish as I asked?'

'Yes, dear.'

'And you remembered to replace the loose stickers?'

'Of course, dear.'

Old Park lay some five miles north of town on the new by-pass. Vernon adjusted his sunglasses and gently squeezed pressure onto the accelerator. Now, for the first time in the race, he had Schumacher and his flying Ferrari in his sights. He cruised effortlessly onto the tail of the red menace. He could hear the roar of the crowd urging him on. He glanced at the cascade of Union Jacks waving their salute. Vernon made up his mind: he would overtake on the home straight just as they came out of the Paddock Wood chicane. Only one more circuit of the race left and he *had* to finish in first place to snatch the world championship from Schumacher.

'Not too close, Vernon, and for goodness' sake slow down. You did realise you were doing sixty miles an hour up by Thripps copse. You know full well that I get car sick if you go too fast. Have some consideration, please!'

'Sorry, dear.' He reduced his speed and could only look on as the red Ferrari disappeared into the sunset.

'Here it is, Vernon! Look, you've gone past it now. What's the matter with you, man?'

Vernon checked his rear view mirror and reversed into the turning for Old Park.

'You've got that far away look on your face again Vernon. I just don't know what's got into you lately.'

'Sorry, dear.' He pulled up outside the Old Park bowls

club, and while his wife struggled to get out of her seat he retrieved her bowls bag and trolley from the boot.

'Now don't forget I shall be ready to be picked up at about six o'clock.'

'Yes, dear.'

'You won't forget, will you?'

'No, dear.'

They parted without a flicker of affection – no looking back or waving. Back on the by-pass he slammed his foot down again; perhaps he would be given one more chance. Yes, there ahead he could see the fiery red Ferrari. He must have been in for a pit stop, perhaps a new set of tyres. Now it would be all or nothing. He felt the adrenalin rush through his whole body. In his quest to overtake his adversary he failed to register the give way signs at Cross Levels. Only too late did he realise that cars were approaching from both directions. He froze in fear as he realised his mistake. By some miracle, involving the screeching of tyres and blowing of horns, they managed to avoid him. He slowed down, his whole body shaking. He could have been killed; what's worse, he could have killed somebody. The headlines flashed through his mind: 'Mangled bodies in by-pass pile up!' For the next three miles he crept cautiously along at thirty miles an hour, completely unaware of the build up of impatient motorists at his rear.

He sat in the car park of Staverly bowls club for ten minutes, relieved that his body had finally stopped shaking. He dabbed the sweat from his forehead. Perhaps his wife was right after all. It wouldn't do any harm to have the doctor check him over. He had to admit he hadn't felt quite his usual self of late.

He collected his bowls from the boot of the car and made his way into the clubhouse, hardly aware of the greetings from other team members. He presented himself to the team captain.

'Vernon Spratt,' he mumbled, 'all present and correct.'

'Hello, Vernon,' said the captain, looking up from the table holding the team sheets. 'Already got you down, Vernon. Always the first name to go down. You've never disappointed yet.' He smiled and handed Vernon the score card. 'I expect we'll get another work of art. You put the others to shame – can hardly decipher some of them.' He looked up at Vernon then and said with some concern, 'You all right old chap? Look a bit under the weather, if you ask me.'

Vernon heard himself mumbling some sort of reply, although for the life of him he couldn't remember what. He felt somehow detached from reality, not quite with it. He put it down to delayed shock after his narrow escape at the crossroads. He still couldn't get the noise of the blaring horns and screeching tyres out of his head.

The game itself seemed to pass in fits and starts. There were times when everything appeared brightly lit up, as if in a spotlight. During these brief spells he played some of the best bowls of his life, getting both his woods on the jack and accepting the accolades that followed. Then there were darker, woollier times when he couldn't remember if he had played his woods or not. After the eleventh end, in one of the brighter, more lucid spells, he focused on his scorecard with absolute horror. The first half dozen scores had been entered in his usual beautifully inscribed lettering. The following three scores looked as though a completely foreign hand had taken over. But it was the final two entries that made him blink in horror and amazement. Barely legible, they could have been scribbled by a child of two or three years only.

He panicked. He had never handed in such an illegible scorecard in his life. What would the captain say? He gazed at the far end of the rink to check the scoreboard, but the sun blinded him. He shielded his eyes with his hands and located the scoreboard, only to find it jumping about to evade his questioning gaze. The scoreboard ceased its jumping, but then all the numbers twisted over and over until they became a complete blur. In the middle of a sunny afternoon he felt an icy-cold sweat creep over his body. He heard a voice talking to him as if from a long way off.

'Come on, Vernon old chap. It's your shot.' The voice slowed down and deepened as if coming from a gramophone that needed winding up. 'We've nothing in the head, Vernon. Give it your best.'

Vernon picked up a wood. It felt like a cannon ball. He didn't know if it was his wood or not. He gathered his feet together on the mat, hoping he was at least facing in the right direction. Ahead of him people in white moved about in slow motion as in some ghostly vision. He drew his arm back in the act of delivering the wood, but it seemed to be slipping from his grasp. He felt his body falling forward. A diaphanous curtain of red mist spread in front of his eyes, mixed with shafts of light brighter than he had ever seen before. As his head hit the ground illuminated rockets exploded in all directions.

At Old Park the mid-afternoon sun shone just as brightly. Through the gaps in the willow trees it glinted on the brook that meandered around the outskirts of the park. In the play area young children ran about shouting excitedly as they slid down the slides and swung in unison on the swings. On the bowling green Gertrude Spratt was enjoying herself as much as any of the children.

Her rink, with only two ends left to play, were holding an incredible thirty-seven shots to nil advantage. Never before in her bowling career had she led a victorious rink in a complete whitewash. She herself was playing out of her skin. Several times she had turned a losing situation, sometimes four or five shots down, into winning ends with her skill. On the penultimate end, with her two woods to come, they held a two shot advantage. By the time she had played her woods it had increased to four. One end to go. She urged her ladies on for one final effort. She felt so invigorated, full of life and energy. It was as if all the superfluous weight wrapped around her body had dropped off and she was back to the sprightly seven stones of her early teenage years. The ladies didn't let her down; spurred on by her confident commands and directions they rose to the occasion. By the time they had crossed over, with only the two skips to play, Old Park found themselves another six shots down. Woeful looks crossed their faces at the prospect of an almighty hammering. They might even lose the last end to a full house of eight shots.

Playing her first wood with calm and measured authority Gertrude succeeded in adding a seventh shot into the head. The wood also collected the added bonus of finishing in such a position as to protect the head from an opponent's drive, the only possible shot that could damage the end. After the ladies had finished their gleeful dance, Gertrude looked up with satisfaction as her number three held up seven fingers. She collected her thoughts, took three deep breaths and prepared to draw one more shot before an excited but hushed audience. A split second before letting go of her wood the telephone in the clubhouse rang, the sound passing through the outside extension and reverberating like a death rattle around the rinks. That brief interruption shattered Gertrude's concentration. She could only watch in horror as her wood passed at least a yard wide of her intended position. It swung in off its bias, clattered off two opposing woods and knocked the jack back to the wide open spaces short of the ditch. A gasp of disbelief arose from Gertrude's team. The lead and second turned away, their hands covering dismayed faces.

Her number three slowly surveyed the transformed head until she indicated with four fingers held downwards.

Gertrude threw her duster down in disgust. 'That bloody telephone!' she cursed, loud enough for everyone on the greens to raise their heads in amazement. Such goings on! A murmuring and pointing of fingers followed her every move until she realised the seriousness of the sin she had committed.

'It's only a game,' commented her opponent.

After all, she had suffered with graceful dignity the humiliation of end after end of combative bowling.

Gertrude offered her hand in apology. 'Yes, of course. You're quite right, my dear. I'm extremely sorry – just got carried away in the heat of the moment. But what an inopportune time for that cursed telephone to ring.'

'Yes. Most unfortunate for you, I admit, but at least I can go into tea without a zero on my scorecard. I don't think I could have lived that down.'

A loud voice followed through on the public address system: 'Urgent telephone call for Mrs Gertrude Spratt. Please report to the clubhouse as soon as possible!'

The word 'urgently' struck a vulnerable chord in Gertrude's heart. It filled her for some strange reason, with a feeling of impending doom. She could find no focus for it, however. She had no relations or family within the nearest six counties, so it would be highly unlikely for anyone to descend on her without warning. The only two things important to her in her closed life were Pinky and Vernon. Pinky had been left curled peacefully up in his basket and he very rarely bothered to move himself. So it *had* to be Vernon. He had seemed to be in a bit of a dither lately, forgetting things and daydreaming. Then, strangely, he had bought her a bunch of beautiful red roses for no reason she could think of. It wasn't her birthday or their wedding anniversary. Just a bunch of beautiful flowers with a card attached in his copperplate writing, saying simply: 'Love, Vernon'. She knew him to be a man of few words and barely demonstrative of his so called love. But there existed an unmentioned bond between them, one unnoticed by the outside world. The box of luxury Belgian chocolates he bought for her and placed on her pillow when she awoke on a Sunday morning was a manifestation of this. While she enjoyed the luxury of a lie-in, fuelled by her delights, Vernon would be up and about, taking Pinky for his early morning walk before returning to prepare breakfast.

These thoughts passed haphazardly through her mind. It must be Vernon, she concluded. Perhaps he's pranged the car or had some other minor accident. That would assume enormous importance in Vernon's mind; he wouldn't want to let her down by leaving her stranded. He may have phoned to forewarn her, so that she wouldn't jump at him like a bull at a gate. She decided she would chastise him only lightly, explain to him that it was only a car and could be repaired. The relief on his face would be a joy to behold. If his daydreaming proved to have been responsible for the accident occurred she would straightaway insist on an appointment with the doctor. The smile and spirit returned to her face as she could hear him saying, 'Yes, dear' in that familiar flat monotone of his.

On entering the clubhouse her eyes fell immediately on the receiver lying on the desk in the green steward's office. She imagined Vernon on the other end, nervously summoning up courage to excuse his errant behaviour. But the voice on the other end could not have been more different from her husband's nor more business-like.

'Mrs Spratt?'

'Speaking.'

'Mrs Gertrude Emily Spratt of fifty-four, Downsway, Belvington?'

'Yes, that's me.'

'This is Police Sergeant Burnett of Belvington Police. Are you the wife of Vernon Norman Spratt of the same address?'

'Yes, of course. What's happened to him?'

'I'm sorry, Mrs Spratt. We have to make sure we are speaking to exactly the right person in these circumstances. We do not like to make mistakes in these cases.'

'What do you mean, officer?' Gertrude felt the hairs on the nape of her neck beginning to rise. 'Has he had an accident of some sort?'

'No, madam, he has not been involved in any accident.'

Gertrude breathed out a long sigh of relief and dabbed at the perspiration on her forehead. 'What's the fool been up to then?' she thought. Fancy getting her all worked up like this.

'Now, madam, are you sitting down? Because I want to prepare you for some bad news.' The officer cleared his throat. 'Your husband was rushed to the county hospital at approximately four thirty this afternoon.'

'The hospital? What happened to him?' Gertrude could hear her voice rising. Suddenly, she felt sick in her stomach. 'Is he all right?'

'I'm not quite sure, madam, but our latest information is that he's in a very critical condition. You need to get there as quickly as possible. We have arranged a patrol car to come and pick you up. But I'm afraid the hospital has told us to prepare you for the worst. As I say, the patrol car should be with you in a matter of minutes.'

Mrs Spratt heard the click of the receiver being replaced. She felt the hand piece drop away from her and clatter onto the wooden table. She could do nothing to stop herself from stumbling backward and collapsing in a heap in the corner of the office.

The trip to the hospital felt like the longest journey she

170

had ever embarked upon, although the actual distance was less than five miles. The two young police officers spoke softly to each other, or into their radio to give the expected time of arrival. She heard them receiving further instructions to attend to a domestic incident after dropping her off at the hospital. When the traffic built up they switched on the flashing light and the siren and she marvelled as the traffic parted before them like a miracle.

On her arrival at the hospital she was calmly ushered through to the inner portals of the accident and emergency department by an efficient young lady from reception. Her spirits were lifted by the lack of hurry in her companion's footsteps. Just a calm stroll, as though this were an everyday occurrence – which, of course, it was. The young lady showed her into a small private waiting room with a desk and no more than two or three chairs. When she tried to ask what was happening the young lady averted her eyes and explained that she would tell the doctor she had arrived. Gertrude tried to convince herself that this was a good omen. If her poor Vernon lay in imminent danger surely she would have been rushed straight to his bedside. She composed herself, patting her neatly styled hair back into place. Trembling hands straightened her jacket and brushed down her skirt. Only then did she realise she was still in full bowling gear. What a queer sight she must have looked. No time for changing in the accident and emergency department; people were fighting life and death battles.

The door opened and a young doctor, tall and thin, and with a battle-glazed look in his eyes made a slow deliberate act of closing the door. He glanced at Gertrude to see if she could recognise the look of death behind his tortoise-shell framed spectacles. Gertrude noticed his eyes move slightly to avoid full contact, and in that fleeting instant she knew she was too late.

'Are you on your own?' asked the doctor, a trace of

nervousness in his voice. He no doubt had to carry out this onerous task many times in the course of his work, but that did not make it any easier.

Gertrude nodded slightly and twisted the handkerchief round and round in her hands.

'I'm afraid it's bad news.'

She fought to control the frightened whimper that escaped her trembling lips. The doctor knelt down in front of her and held her hands.

'I'm sorry. There was little we could do for him. He was dead on arrival. If it's any comfort for you at all he would probably have been dead before he hit the ground. He suffered a massive brain haemorrhage, you see. You have to understand that sometimes these occur so suddenly there's virtually no warning.'

Her whole body convulsed and she emitted such a scream of despair that even the doctor was taken aback. Just as quickly the outburst subsided, as though the emotion had fled from her body in one fell swoop. She calmed down and dabbed at her eyes with her handkerchief.

'Do you know, I had a funny feeling something was wrong with him. I told him to have a check up, but he just wouldn't listen. Stubborn as a mule.'

The doctor smiled reassuringly, relieved that he had got through the worst part of his job. 'Were there any symptoms? Anything out of the ordinary you can describe?'

'Well, symptoms no; I could hardly call them that. Just sort of funny things you pick up on. You know, daydreaming, his mind not on the job. Then he would do something unexpected and surprise me.'

The doctor rose to his feet. 'Sounds like the classic symptoms – extreme changes in personality. It's the slow build up of pressure in the brain. It can manifest itself in many ways.'

'Can I see him?'

'Not at the moment. I wouldn't advise it. Not to put too fine a point on it a haemorrhage is not a pleasant thing. The nurses are in there with him. You can see him later on. I suggest you get in touch with someone who can come and collect you, stay with you for a little while. You may experience some sort of delayed shock. I'll send a nurse in so she can take all your details.'

On the days leading up to the funeral Gertrude struggled to come to terms with the loss of her husband. She recalled that before his death she had contemplated how she would cope if he were the first to pass away. To tell the truth, she felt as though she had been robbed – no, cheated perhaps. It's difficult to find the right word in these circumstances. The first to go – well, their life is over – finished. Surely she had the advantage of life to cling on to. But it is difficult when you are left with the grieving and have to pick up the shattered pieces of your life alone. You still have to feed yourself, dress yourself and put on a brave face. You have to chase the demons out of your mind and try to get some sleep.

With Vernon being such a quiet, private man she would have thought that living without him would not be too difficult. She discovered that she missed him much more than if he had been a loud, brash, indifferent man. She just missed having him about her. He had spoilt her in so many ways, especially as things became more difficult with her ever-increasing weight. Who would present her with chocolates now? It wasn't the same, having to buy them yourself.

Pinky moped and brooded about the house. He followed her about from room to room getting under her feet. Gertrude found herself unable to open her husband's wardrobe, or to move his toiletries from the bathroom. She sat at the writing bureau, looking at his collections of pens standing neatly in their holders. Such a quiet, simple man, who was happy with the basic, simple things in life. How could he have known he would have such an effect on her whole being?

Gertrude thought that his funeral would be a quiet affair but was pleasantly surprised to find people still filing into the church as his coffin arrived. Friends from the bowling fraternity stood proudly side by side in their club blazers to pay their last respects. In his quiet, sincere way he had penetrated more lives than she had thought possible. The only person Gertrude felt able to confide in was his younger sister Janet, a quiet, reflective spinster, very similar in many ways to her brother. She said that Vernon had often told her that he was a very happy man in a very fulfilling marriage, and that each loved the other in their own particular ways. He considered himself to be a very fortunate man to have found the company of such a special woman.

Two days after the funeral Gertrude had made up her mind. She had not eaten a single chocolate since Vernon's death. She carried the last box of chocolates he had bought her out into the garden and made herself comfortable on the wooden bench. The sun had just started to sink down between the poplar trees. Her fingers slowly traced the selection in the box. She worked out that if she took two painkillers to every chocolate she would finish both boxes simultaneously. She started with her favourite: feuille d'orange – orange flavoured crème, covered in milk chocolate.

10

Does My Posterior Look Large in This?

The short, hirsute body of Charles Boniface stumbled somewhat bleary-eyed into the bathroom just as the village clock majestically struck the seventh hour. The smallish chamber facing in north-east normally afforded insufficient light at the best of times. Today it felt almost claustrophobic, festooned as it was with an abundance of female apparel. Hanging grimly on three lines suspended over the enamel bath were at least half a dozen pairs of tights. They varied from a light tan with support to the darkest shade of brown conceived, capable of hiding advanced cases of cellulite, varicose veins, wrinkles and anything else that mother nature could cruelly throw at the female form. Accompanying them were myriad slips and petticoats in a rainbow of colours from a loud pink to a deep blue, adorned with petite hearts and bows embroidered in silver satin. Draped casually over the radiator were several sets of brassières. The two largest of these, if coupled together, would be quite capable of transporting Charles' set of size six, heavy, hensulite bowls.

To Mr Boniface, just donning any of this attire, never mind flouncing about in it all day, was beyond comprehension. Little did he realise that before today's sun dropped out of the sky his whole body would be incarcerated in these alien vestments.

He bathed languidly without becoming entangled in any

of the washing. Shaving, however, turned out to be less than successful. While dodging a swaying panty girdle he accidentally cut himself on the point of his chin.

Ablutions finally completed without further injury, he sat himself at the breakfast table and waited for the human stereophonic system to switch on.

'Managed to cut yourself again, darling?' commented his wife, Betty, cutting a small square off the paper towel and sticking it crudely on the congealing blood.

'He must be the clumsiest shaver in the world,' declared Connie, the elder of the sisters by some two years. Her long, sheepish face was illuminated by darting blue eyes. She addressed Charles mostly through her sister, hardly ever directly. 'What's he using these days? A broken bottle?'

Betty carefully poured thick strong tea into three breakfast mugs. 'I bought him a brand new safety razor for his birthday, but I suppose he couldn't fathom out how to switch the safety catch on,' she muttered.

'It doesn't have a safety catch,' corrected Charles stirring in three spoonfuls of sugar. 'You only find safety catches on automatic firearms and other dangerous equipment.'

'Well, why do they call them safety razors? Perhaps we could sue them under the Trade Descriptions Act,' challenged Betty, never the one to be bettered in an argument.

'My dear departed Wilfred had a cut-throat razor for over thirty-five years and never cut himself once,' boasted Connie.

'Your precious Wilfred, if I remember rightly had a full beard and moustache for over thirty-five years. He was too lazy to shave.'

'Oh, so he did,' admitted Connie, gently laughing to herself. 'I'll see if I can find it though. Perhaps your Charlie can use it.'

'If he can gouge lumps off his face with a safety razor,

176

heaven forbid we let him loose with a cut-throat. He's likely to use it literally.' Betty shovelled toast onto a plate like a navvy laying paving slabs.

'In that case I'll definitely have a look for it,' cackled Connie.

This playful banter washed over Charles like gravy over newly roasted potatoes. He had endured it now for some fifteen years, ever since Connie's husband, Wilf, fell off the back of a coal wagon. It wasn't the fall that killed him; he had the misfortune to roll into the path of a coach carrying a group of pensioners to their weekly bingo game. They had been extremely upset, not so much about the accident but at the loss of a night's entertainment at the Palais de Bingo. The coal company involved was not happy about the tragic state of affairs either because two bags of nutty slack mysteriously disappeared from the scene of the accident.

So, for the past decade-and-a-half, Charles had had to come to terms with a female dominated household. Rainy days were the worst: the washing couldn't be hung out to dry naturally in the gentle breeze which accounted for the festooned bathroom. He couldn't recall the room being so full of women's undergarments since Connie had put Exlax in her chocolate and walnut cake by mistake.

'What time did you say your bowls match was?' he asked, leaning back and pushing away his breakfast plates.

'Ten-thirty, sharp. I've told you twice already. Now where was I? Connie, I think you'd better put your surgical support stockings on. It will be murder walking up and down the greens if the wind doesn't drop.' Betty glanced apprehensively out of the window to observe a fresh south-easterly stirring the tops of the conifers and causing what remained of the tulips and daffodils to dance to and fro as if joining in a Gay Gordon.

The match in question was the semi-final of the town's

ladies' rinks. Betty Boniface and her team were up against her arch rival, Linda Potter Brown, and her ladies from Bourne Park – a rival who had comprehensively beaten her three times in the last three years. A prestigious place in the town final had always been Betty's burning ambition and this was the closest she had progressed so far.

This season's team of lead, Mabel Pinkerton, two, Doris Dewhurst, and sister Connie at number three, didn't exactly fill her with overwhelming confidence. She had skipped far stronger personnel. The unfortunate fact that both Connie and Mabel suffered from bow legs and that Doris had knock knees meant that when they lined up together they spelt OXO – a circumstance more in keeping with a comedy act than a bowling team. However, if their limbs were not their strongest point, Betty felt in her bones that lady luck was smiling on them this year. They had enjoyed some spectacular shots and wicks in preliminary matches and she was determined nothing would stand in her way.

While Charles busied himself washing up the breakfast dishes, the sisters applied their war paint and donned their bowling attire. He complimented them on their appearance, while inwardly admitting that a full strength ladies' rink kitted up and ready for battle always put the fear of God into him.

Betty brushed at the sleeve of her blazer. 'It doesn't take much effort to keep up a smart appearance. I've always found that if you look good and feel good it enhances your playing ability. I don't condone any slacking on my rinks, do I, Connie?'

'Of course not, love,' replied Connie, struggling to fix her hat without disturbing her hair.

'It's not right,' said Betty shaking her head. 'It looks more like a flower pot than a hat.' She straightened it, then jammed it on hard.

'I can't think if it's too tight,' protested Connie. 'My brain can't breathe.'

'If you had half a brain you'd be considered dangerous,' cajoled Betty, finally giving her sister the 'all clear'.

Since her husband's demise, Betty felt Connie had let her ambitions slide somewhat. There were still plenty of available bachelors or widowers who, if worked upon, might be considered commercially acceptable prospects. Some could walk unaided, some could see unaided and some could hear unaided. Admittedly, she had yet to stumble upon anyone who enjoyed the benefit of all three working faculties. If she did, Betty's matrimonial services could be brought immediately into play. Only recently her high hopes of a match had been cruelly crushed when Billy Toggs joined the bowls club. He enjoyed the rare benefit of all three functioning faculties and Betty wasted little time in inviting him for Sunday lunch to meet her sister. Nothing special, mind – just some cold meats, pickles and summer salad, with homemade chocolate and walnut cake (without the Exlax, of course) for dessert. However, Billy Toggs's rather athletic dives into the bathroom, no fewer than five times during the course of the meal, convinced Betty that incontinence would place a severe strain on any romantic assignations with Connie.

Their arrival at Piddingly bowls club that morning was greeted by song thrushes and blackbirds diving in and out of the ornamental bushes. They were also greeted by Tom Bartley, green steward, cleaner and general dogsbody. A small, sinewy man and a confirmed bachelor, he appeared to live permanently in his club blazer, which consequently looked a little the worse for wear. Tom was always the first person at the clubhouse. Whether you arrived at ten o'clock, eight o'clock, or just after daybreak he would be there. The majority of club members suspected he lived on the premises. He even had the audacity to give his address and telephone number as that of the club. When questioned about such matters, his answer was that he spent more time at the club than at home. As the greens were kept in pristine condition and the clubhouse immaculate, nobody felt inclined to object. After all the post was entirely voluntary, and he received only an end of season gratuity.

On this sunny morning he stood defiantly at the entrance, his green stewards' badge hanging from his lapel like a sheriff's badge, challenging all-comers. The official club badge had long since been discarded on the grounds of insignificance. The one Tom had personally made up measured a glorious six inches by three and was of a holographic design. The reflective angles displayed either 'Green Steward' or 'Thomas Bartley Esq.' You took your choice.

'Good morning, Mrs Boniface,' said Tom without a flicker of emotion. He always welcomed people he didn't much care for by their surnames. 'Morning, Connie,' he winked. 'Morning, Charles.'

The adversaries stood facing each other like guards at a border crossing.

'Season tickets, please!' demanded Tom, his chest compelling his blazer to expand by at least three inches.

'Come on, Tom,' said Charles. 'Surely we don't have to go through this rigmarole every time? You know we're members.'

Tom made a great show of selecting one of his several keys on a long silver chain attached to his belt. Turning his back on them he locked the clubhouse door.

'More than my job's worth to admit people without tickets or other methods of payment.'

Charles felt inclined to explain that nobody would have his job if they paid them but, like the two ladies, took the line of least resistance and produced his season ticket.

'All present and correct,' smiled Tom triumphantly. He executed another flamboyant flashing of the keys before returning the chain to his belt. 'Please enjoy the facilities and leave them as you would expect to find them. I've put you on rink number one.'

Connie glanced at the other vacant rinks and shook her head. 'Oh no! Any rink but number one.'

'What's wrong with it?' asked Tom.

'Well, it's right next to the gents' toilet for a start. If the wind's blowing in the right direction you can get a strange aroma at times. Brings on my hayfever something chronic.'

'I can assure you, madam, I cleaned out the gentlemen's conveniences this very morning. I polished the seats, attacked the S bends with Harpic and disinfected the urinals to the highest standards. Even His Holiness the Pope would be pleased to have a p...'

'Yes, Mr Bartley, I'm quite sure you're right,' intervened Betty. 'Nobody is questioning your cleaning abilities. But would you mind if we moved to another rink? They are all free, I take it?'

'Yes. But if you think I'm moving the mats and scoreboard around willy-nilly you've got another think coming.'

'Thank you, Tom. I'll move them over,' said Charles.

Tom contemplated the bowlers and then the clubhouse, as if leaving them would be inviting trouble. 'Well, I'm off to get my cigarettes and morning paper. I hope I can trust you to keep an eye on the place.'

'Go on with you,' replied Charles, trying out the different chairs for comfort. 'I'm not doing anything for a couple of hours.' He had hardly made himself comfortable when the phone rang. The door flew open and the green steward hurtled back into the room and snatched the phone out of Charles's grasp.

He straightened his blazer, polished his badge and answered: 'Thomas Bartley, green steward, Piddingly bowls club.' He hummed a few times, nodded his head and finished with, 'Certainly sir.' He waved to Betty. 'It's for you. Reg Dewhurst on the line. Seems to be in a state of agitation.'

Betty dashed over, a worried look on her face. 'I hope there's nothing wrong with Doris. I thought she was cutting it a bit fine – she's usually the first one here. Hello, Reg. Everything all right? What do you mean, you "don't think Doris can make it"? Has she had an accident? She has? What do you mean, "of sorts"?'

'Oh dear,' said Connie, catching Charles' eye. 'That's scuppered our chances if Doris can't make it. Your Betty will be like a bear with a sore head.'

'Tell me about it,' moaned Charles. He saw that the next few hours in the Boniface household would be as agitated and stressful as throwing Christians to the lions.

'Spell it out, Reg. You're not making much sense. Is the accident life threatening? Have you called an ambulance? What do you mean, you're "too embarrassed to"? Doris was in the bathroom when you heard an almighty scream? She was in some sort of fit? What happened, Reg? Spit it out. What are you laughing for? Hit the nail on the head? Stop talking in riddles. She found out she'd been cleaning her teeth with your haemorrhoid cream? You left the tube in the toothpaste mug by mistake after applying it to your pi... Reg, I don't think I want to know that. What's she doing now? She's sitting on the lavatory seat but she can't speak because she's frothing at the mouth and her lips are puckering up?'

Betty slammed the phone down and let out a bloodcurdling scream. Connie stood open-mouthed while Charles screwed up his eyes and clamped his hands over his ears.

Mabel Pinkerton, their lead bowler pushed the door open just as the scream reached its crescendo. She glanced nervously at Betty who was now banging her head against the wall.

'Betty in one of her bad moods then?'

182

'You could say that,' replied Charles

'That's not a good omen for the match. She's a difficult enough skip when she's in a good mood. She'll make our lives a misery out there.'

Betty calmed down somewhat and sank into one of the chairs. 'Hello, Mabel. Could have saved you a wasted journey. Doris has let us down ... let us down in our hour of need.'

Mabel fiddled with the buckle on her new pink mackintosh. 'What's the matter with her? It's not like Doris to let us down. Has there been a bereavement?'

'No, not yet, but when I get my hands on Doris's husband there will be. She's only gone and brushed her teeth with his haemorrhoid cream by mistake.'

'Yuk! I think I'm going to faint.'

'Don't you dare, Mabel Pinkerton. We're one down already, don't go and make matters worse. I see you've been down the charity shops again.'

'What do you mean?'

'That horrible pink mackintosh. It's revolting.'

'Do you mind? It's brand new!'

Connie began untying her shoes and putting them back into her bowls bag.

'Still, it explains one mystery. I always thought that Reg Dewhurst had a funny walk. Had him down as a bit of a nancy boy.'

Betty stood up and began prowling round the room. 'It's no good, we'll just have to find a replacement.'

'Fat chance,' said Connie. 'By the time we phone up and find somebody willing and able it will be too late. That Linda Porter-Brown will claim the match if you're more than ten minutes late.'

Betty put her head in her hands. 'She's going to do me

for the fourth year running, I'll never get a better chance. I've fought tooth and nail to reach the semi-finals only to be beaten by a tube of haemorrhoid cream.'

'Talk about piling on the agony,' taunted Charles with a smirk on his face.

'That's not in the least bit funny. If all you can do is crack infantile jokes about a serious situation...' Betty's voice trailed off. Her expression changed. 'Hang on a minute! I've got it ... it's staring me in the face.'

'What is?' asked Charles. He didn't like it when his wife announced sudden brainstorms. It usually meant trouble.

'Not *what* ... who? You, of course. How many people in this room?'

'Four,' replied Mabel in bewilderment. 'We three and Charles.'

'Wrong,' said Betty, pulling Charles out of his chair. 'Four women – a complete rink if we turn Charles into Doris Dewhurst.'

Charles made a beeline for the door. 'You're raving mad, woman, if you think I'm changing sex for you. I've never worn women's clothes in my life and I don't intend to start now.'

Betty frogmarched her husband back into the room. 'Now, Charles, don't be too hasty. If I remember rightly you owe me one or two favours.'

'I do?'

'Yes. Remember when you put your back out? Who helped you in and out of your underwear? What about when you broke your false teeth on one of Connie's rock cakes. Who made your favourite leek and faggot soup? Yes, you owe me big time. Quick, girls! Have a look in the ladies' changing room. See if we can find something to dress him up in.'

'You're not seriously trying to replace Doris with Charles?' gasped Mabel.

184

'We'll never get away with it in a million years. He doesn't look even remotely like a woman,' protested Connie. 'We can try ... we can at least try. He'll be all right as long as he keeps his mouth shut,' said Betty, poking about in the lost property box. 'Look! Here's a cravat for a start.' She pulled Charles's tie off and clipped on the cravat. Charles moved to yank it off. 'If you don't do this for me and the girls I'll never forgive you. I'll make your life a misery, and you can forget about ordering that new snooker cue signed by Hurricane Higgins with a book of accompanying instructions.'

Mabel dashed out of the changing room holding a skirt and hat in her hands.

'The skirt looks a bit long and the hat's a bit battered. What do you think?'

Betty pushed her husband into the men's changing room and practically tore his trousers off.

Charles froze. 'I'm keeping my underpants on. No way am I wearing knickers.'

'Nobody's asking you to. That would be too devious. You're not meant to enjoy it, just endure it.' She fixed up the skirt, stuck the hat on his bald head and pushed him out of the room. The skirt ended mid-calf, revealing a length of hairy leg and size ten suede boots.

'He looks like a pantomime dame,' said Connie.

'He looks bloody ridiculous, if you'll pardon my French,' commented Mabel. 'We'll never get away with it.'

'All right,' flustered Betty. 'It's only the first show. I'll admit there's room for improvement. Take your shoes and socks off and slip your bowls shoes on.'

Charles shuffled to his locker and did as he was told. The improvement was nugatory.

'Why do you have such big feet and hairy legs?' complained

Betty. 'I think you're being awkward on purpose. Have a look round, girls, see if we can find some tights.'

'I know where there's some,' said Connie. Moments later she emerged from the ladies' toilet holding two stockings. 'They're not exactly a matching pair – one's beige and the other's brown. They were wrapped around the hot water pipe.'

'Put them on, quick – we haven't got much time,' ordered Betty. Charles put up a struggle but the women held him down and slipped the stockings over his hairy legs. They finished six inches above his knees, but when he stood up they finished in a wrinkled heap around his ankles.

'There's a stapler in the office,' suggested Connie. The colour drained rapidly from Charles's face.

'I think two elastic bands will suffice,' said Betty. They stood him in front of the mirror.

'He doesn't look too bad from the waist down,' said Mabel, squinting through half-closed eyes. 'But the top half is lacking something: he's got no bosom.'

'I'm not wearing a bra, so don't get any bright ideas,' Charles remonstrated.

'There's a black bra hanging from the door handle. Sandra Makepeace uses it for collecting the raffle money in,' offered Connie. Betty found two tea towels, squashed them into round balls, stuffed them into the bra and fastened over Charles's hairy chest.

'I can hardly breathe,' gasped Charles.

'They are not meant to be comfortable. Now you know what *we* have to endure,' explained Connie, regarding him critically. 'The short sleeves and the hairy arms lack a certain femininity. Why does he have to be so hairy? Hairy arms. Hairy legs. The only place he hasn't got any hair is on his head.'

'I told you he does his best to be awkward,' said Betty. 'And that hat's far too small. It looks like a blistered pimple

186

on his head. Swap hats with him Mabel; you've got the biggest head.'

'Pardon?'

'You know what I mean,' snapped Betty.

'But my hat's brand new; my husband bought it as an anniversary present. I don't think he would approve if he knew it had been gracing Charles' greasy head.'

'Don't be such a moaner; it's only for one game. You lend him your hat and I'll lend him my white cardigan. At least it will cover up his hairy arms.'

They paraded Charles once more in front of the mirror.

'It's nearly there,' said Betty.

'It's no oil painting,' commented Connie.

'It's his face,' said Mabel. 'He's pig ugly.'

'Do you mind? That's my husband you're talking about. There's no need to get personal.'

'Well, you said I had a big head.'

'No I never. I meant you've got the biggest hat; that's not the same. Makeup.'

'Well, I will if you will – but you started it.'

'No, woman, I mean 'make up'. That's what's missing. Some of my foundation, powder and lipstick. That will finish the job.'

'You'll need a fair sized trowel to fill in his cracks and crevices,' remarked Connie. 'He didn't exactly shave himself as smooth as a baby's bottom this morning.'

Strong arms held Charles rigid while the foundation and powder were lavishly administered. They rouged his cheeks and applied cherry-red lipstick. Connie completed the masterpiece with one of her trademark beauty spots. They contemplated the monster they had created.

'Rubbish,' commented Mabel.

'I've seen a lot worse at the 'Grab a Granny' night in The Rat and Ferret,' admitted Connie.

Betty eyed her sister with a certain amount of suspicion.

She had always been led to believe that she frequented the genteel tea dances for the over sixties in the lounge bar of the Royal Hotel. 'It will have to do. Just remember to keep your mouth shut. Pretend you're hard of hearing or you've been struck dumb.'

Charles bent over with some difficulty to practise his bowls delivery.

'Does my posterior look large in this?'

Mabel and Connie collapsed into each other's arms, but Betty failed to see the funny side.

'Of course it will if you stomp up and down like a navvy on a building site. Show a bit of decorum.'

Charles put his hands on his hips and gyrated like an old queen at a transvestite's coming out ball. All three women collapsed in hysterics.

'If only I had my camcorder,' sighed Mabel. 'Nobody will ever believe this.'

The quartet was swiftly brought back to reality by the sight of Linda Porter-Brown and her Bourne Park team entering the clubhouse. Immaculately turned out in maroon and green jackets they surveyed the surroundings and their opponents with barely concealed disdain.

'Hello, Betty,' said Linda, sizing up her foes and fundamentally dismissing them as 'also rans' – a rough looking bunch, especially the two who had enough make up on to be in a circus. 'Didn't see you in any of the town finals last year. Hoping for better luck this season, are we?'

Betty returned the greeting with a stifled half smile, half sneer.

'Nice to see you and the girls again, Linda. Carrying a trifle extra weight this year, are we? Let's hope it doesn't affect your performance too much. We'll play on rink number four, if you've no objections.'

She led the players outside, past the commemorative flower beds newly planted with geraniums and nasturtiums. Glancing round, she was just in time to see her husband walking a little uncertainly swinging his own pair of woods.

She whispered out of the side of her mouth, 'You don't see many ladies playing with a set of size six heavy woods. Change them for something smaller.'

Charles stormed back into the clubhouse, slid his woods under the table and rummaged around for a pair of smaller ones. He threw the string bag over his shoulder and ambled back to the greens, the restrictions of his skirt curtailing his usual striding gait.

Betty kept the introductions as brief as possible. Even so, one or two had cause to inspect their hands after Charles's sausage-like fingers had all but squeezed the life out of them. Everything in the park appeared normal. Grey squirrels chased up and down trees, ducks led their young down the gravel path and into the lake, ladies commenced a genteel game of bowls. The opening ends progressed calmly and fairly evenly as the Bourne Park team came to grips with the unfamiliar rink.

'Doesn't your number two – Mrs Dewhurst is it – possess any shots other than a drive? We haven't had the chance to build up a decent end,' commented Linda, surveying the scattered woods.

'She can be a bit heavy handed, but she is very keen is our Doris.'

The ends proceeded, picking up the pace with little more than one or two shots between the antagonists. The opposing number two commented several times on the weather, her husband's frequent bladder problems and the exorbitant price of cod steaks in the supermarkets. Charles returned her friendly endeavours with a grim, crooked smile, minute spots of foundation flaking off from his bristles.

'I'm afraid you won't get much out of her,' explained Connie, 'she suffers from acute deafness; unfortunately, her hearing aid is in for repair under the manufacturer's guarantee scheme.'

'She does appear to be ... how can I say? ... not quite with us,' sympathised her opponent. 'Still, as long as she is enjoying herself.'

The far away look in Charles's eyes soon disappeared. One of the hazards of Piddingly bowls club's being entrenched in a municipal park was that they were neighbours to an adjoining soccer pitch. Occasionally and without warning, a football would be despatched over the fence and onto the rinks. In this particular instance, a ball bounced directly in front of the bowlers about to measure a closely fought end. Charles (née Doris), recognising the danger and momentarily forgetting her lady-like manners, burst out of the group, trapped the ball perfectly with his right foot, shimmied onto his left and expertly chipped it to the feet of the astonished player who had come in through the gate to retrieve the ball. The brawny youth blinked in disbelief, then broke out into a cheeky grin.

'As soon as you've finished playing marbles, darling, you can come and play with us.'

Charles winked, readjusted his skirt and shuffled back to join his astounded companions.

'Quite a character, your Mrs Dewhurst. I can't say I've come across her before. Where on earth did you find her?' asked Linda.

'Oh, I've known her more years than I care to remember.'

'Bit of an oddball though, isn't she? Doesn't quite look the part. Is she married?'

'Believe it or not, she's been very happily married for thirty years. Went to her anniversary party myself,' said Betty, polishing her wood and trying to drop out of the conversation.

'Well, you do surprise me. Still, I suppose it takes all sorts.'

Betty surprised her even further by despatching her second wood on the forehand to knock Linda's holding shot off the jack, leaving herself with a perfect toucher. Linda offered congratulations through clenched teeth. Betty's beaming smile lasted only halfway down the rink when she discreetly ushered Charles to one side.

'One more stunt like that and I'll have your guts for garters!'

'Sorry. I forgot myself,' said Charles fiddling uncomfortably with his new attire. 'Talking about garters, these elastic bands are killing me. I've got pins and needles. I think they're cutting off the blood supply to my vital parts.'

'I'll cut off your vital parts myself if you don't stop complaining. Try and pull your stockings up – you look like Norah Batty. And tuck your shirt in – everyone can see your hairy back.' She relented a little and gave him an encouraging smile. 'Come on, pet, we've only got a few ends left. We win this match and I'll cook your favourite fish pie for supper.'

Charles heeded the encouragement. He bowled like a

demon, placing his woods close enough to the jack, giving Betty every chance to keep level.

The game continued in this close fought fashion until the last end; all the way down to the wire, seventeen shots each. The excitement spread through Betty's team like a red hot curry, so much so that Mabel put her first wood down on the wrong bias. In an effort to redeem herself she bowled far too wide on her forehand and her final wood finished on the adjoining rink. Her opposite number slid her two woods in unopposed. Betty turned away from the head in disgust.

Charles showed he was made of sterner stuff. He knocked the holding wood away from the jack and, although Bourne Park's number two replaced it with her second, Charles' final wood trailed the jack alongside his first wood.

'Well played, Charles!' shouted Betty in her excitement.

'Charles?' queried Linda Potter-Brown. 'I thought her name was Doris?'

'I meant 'Doris' of course,' blustered Betty. 'Just getting caught up in the heat of the moment.'

The mounting enthusiasm also got the better of Connie. She bounced her first wood into the ground, taking all the strength out of the shot. It finished two yards short of the head. Connie, being an old pro, caught Betty's eye.

'Thought I'd better put a blocker in, protect our lead.' To make up for her shortcomings she gave her last wood every ounce her elderly body could muster. Both skips scrambled hurriedly out of the way to avoid having their ankles rapped.

'Who told you to fire? We're already holding two shots,' shouted Betty, only too relieved that no damage had been done. Under her breath she cursed the lifelong waywardness of her sister.

The Bourne Park's number three drew second shot with a skilfully deceptive backhand. The players crossed over in reverent silence, pausing only briefly to wish their respective skips good luck. Sparrows swooped and chased each other out of the trees. Shouts echoed across the soccer pitch. Splashes of laughter drifted in the still morning air from the boating lake. Four woods remained in this titanic struggle. Who would emerge victorious?

Linda Porter-Brown's first wood finished only inches short of the holding shot. They now had two seconds. Betty's first effort finished jack high but, alas, a good yard right of the counting shots. Linda, having previously gauged the line and length with her first wood, played her second to perfection, pushing Charles' out of the head. The Bourne Park ladies leapt up in ecstatic rapture, kissing and hugging each other. Connie stared incredulously at the head, then signalled despondently that they were three shots down.

Betty strode resolutely up the rink to assess the damage. She studied all the relevant angles and possibilities. Then, her mind made up, she walked confidently back to the mat.

Connie endeavoured to bolster the sinking hearts of the Piddingly ladies. 'If anyone can do it Betty can.'

Charles looked on dejectedly, his fish pie supper about to swim back up the proverbial Swannee.

Betty took her time, standing majestically on the mat. The warm sun caressed her determined face. With her last wood running up the green she turned away in disgust.

'It's going to hit that blocker,' she wailed.

Sure enough, it trundled into Connie's short wood. The Bourne Park ladies resumed their jumping and squealing, albeit only briefly. Their triumphant shouts gradually turned to dismay, as the blocker, which had been hit full on, slowly rolled towards the head. It stopped inches from the shot wood and toppled over with just sufficient strength to nudge out the shot wood. The Bourne Park ladies froze in horror. Mabel and Connie fell into each other's arms and danced a merry jig. Charles looked on in wonder at the head, his fish pie supper saved. At the other end of the rink an elated Betty shook her fist in triumph. Linda Porter-Brown seemed dumbstruck.

Amongst the celebrations and commiserations a trivial episode occurred which changed the whole course of events. In the past, history has shown that the smallest of events can change the course of a life time. A glorious victory can be turned into defeat by an apparently insignificant incident.

In this case, the incident occurred itself as the players were strolling down the rink each congratulating or sympathising with their respective skips. The football being used in the game of soccer on the other side of the fence flew over once again and bounced at some pace in front of the bowlers. Little chance of a simple trap and shimmy this time. Charles sussed it out as instinctively as in his playing days. This required a full-bodied volley. He executed it perfectly, leaping a good yard into the air, making faultless contact with his instep and despatching the ball whence it came. A roar of approval issued from the other side of the fence.

Although this manoeuvre was performed to perfection, the landing lacked a certain grace. Unaccustomed to the constriction of a bowling skirt, Charles failed to engage his landing gear in time, and tumbled over in an unsightly heap. Recalling skills from his younger, more athletic years he saved himself from injury by carrying his momentum forward into two fairly acceptable somersaults.

In the process his hat fell off. Complete loss of hair, however, is not entirely unheard of in elderly women. It can easily be concealed by a wig. However, a breathless, heaving torso proved too much for the buttons on a shirt already overstretched. They flew off in different directions

194

revealing a black lacy brassière stuffed with chequered tea towels and strapped to the hairiest chest ever seen on a woman.

Yet the *coup de grâce* remained to be delivered. As Charles desperately tried to pull his shirt together, the catch on the side of his skirt disintegrated and the garment fell to the floor. It revealed two hairy legs, one encased in a crumpled beige stocking held just above the knee by a yellow elastic band, the other leg sporting a dark brown stocking, laddered from top to toe and supported by a rather fetching green elastic band. The highlight of this fashion nightmare had to be the off-white Y fronts which had slipped their moorings somewhat, allowing a pair of shiny round testicles to be displayed in all their glory.

Two of the Bourne Park ladies fainted on the spot. A third nudged her way gingerly forward to have a closer look – she had been a practising vet in her younger years. She concluded the offending objects were definitely male.

The game was up. The game was lost. A disconsolate Betty begged for forgiveness, which Linda Porter-Brown accepted graciously. She could well afford to be gracious, having snatched victory from the jaws of defeat.

Placing a consoling arm around Betty's crumpled shoulders she said, 'A word of advice, Mrs Boniface – something I learned many years ago. Never put your faith in a short man. You usually find his brains are not too far from his backside.'

11

Friends and Neighbours

The mouth-watering aroma of freshly baked sausage rolls and hot buttered crumpets filled the kitchen of 'Larkspur', a house more commonly known as 21, Larksbury Close. The tranquil *cul-de-sac* was sedately decorated with lilac trees and neatly clipped box hedges. In these agreeable surroundings Mrs Norkette felt more than pleased with her culinary efforts. Perhaps too the evening would be a successful and pleasant surprise. The only ingredient that would turn the night into failure or embarrassment might be the unpredictable behaviour of her husband.

Frank Norkette suffered from what might be called mood swings. In days gone by he would have been described as bombastic, awkward, or self-opinionated, depending on how much strong beer and how many whisky chasers he had thrown down his throat. Mrs Norkette was the one who suffered. She had to pick up the pieces and restore everything to peaceful harmony after he had blown through people's emotions and feelings like a verbal tornado. He wasn't all bad, however. On his good days he could be very good; it was the bad days she tried to forget about as quickly as possible. She had to admit that Frank Norkette could make new friends as quickly as the next man. Hanging on to them was his Achilles' heel. Apparently, down at the bowls club he frequented – as much for the cheap alcoholic refreshment as the game itself – he was both popular and

197

unpopular in equal measure, so you can draw your own conclusions from that.

The couple from the aforementioned bowls club, whom Frank had invited round this evening for nibbles and Trivial Pursuit were new to her. She did so hope they were nice people. She liked nothing better than to make new acquaintances and show off her house. Frank, in his mellow moments, showed himself to be an able decorator and had followed her instructions in redesigning their modest home with more or less constructive criticisms. Her penchant for selecting soft furnishings and subtle décor had inspired the majority of visiting relations and friends to compliment her on her style and taste.

Mrs Norkette adjusted the art nouveau mirror in the hallway and separated out the leaves of the *Monstera deliciosa*. First impressions were all-important, and she had just heard the car pull up on the driveway. She instinctively prepared her ears for the two loud blasts Frank always gave on the accelerator to signal his arrival. Why he did it she never understood. It wasn't as if the car could go any further. She removed her apron, gave a final glance around the lounge/diner and prepared to receive her guests. Laughter from the side of the house she interpreted as an encouraging sign. The car doors slammed shut and she waited. She stuck her chest out and pulled her buttocks in. Finally, she brushed at the faintest of creases in her blue woollen two-piece, and still she waited.

'Cooee!' came a voice from the kitchen door. 'Cooee! Mrs Norkette, are you in?'

Mrs Norkette sighed in despair. 'He's only let them in the back way and I haven't cleared the dishes away yet. I might as well not have polished the brass novelty door knocker, I might as well not have a front porch at all.'

'Hello,' offered Mrs Norkette. 'I was expecting my husband to bring you in through the front door, not slide you in round the back like a tradesman.' She greeted her visitor with a gentle hug and a kiss that missed the side of her face by at least three inches.

'The men wandered into the garage and I just sort of followed them. I was directed to the kitchen door by a wave of the hand, as though surplus to their requirements. What a delicious aroma. I do hope you haven't gone to too much trouble.'

Mrs Norkette eyed a woman in her late fifties at a guess, with a slightly weathered face and gentle blue eyes. Her greying hair had been enhanced to a discreet shade of soft blonde. She wore slightly too tight black trousers with a loose fitting black cotton jacket.

'Pleased to meet you, I'm sure. I'm Mrs Norkette, for my sins, and you are?'

'Fanny,' came the strong reply. Her face broke into a generous smile. 'Short for Tiffany, which I haven't been called since the day I got married. And as my husband has always been called Knobby since the day he was born, that's the two of us – Knobby and Fanny. It causes quite a laugh down the bowls club, I can tell you.

'You don't mind?' enquired Mrs Norkette slightly taken aback. 'You must be teased mercilessly.'

'Mind? Oh dear no. I like to think we are both fairly broad minded. It comes in very handy for breaking the ice at parties.'

Mrs Norkette picked up a tray bearing cups, saucers and a floral patterned china teapot and carried them into the lounge/diner. She placed them on the coffee table. It swayed visibly under the weight and she steadied it with her free hand.

'If I've told Frank once to see to this table I've told him a dozen times. Somebody's going to have a nasty accident one of these days, you mark my words. I might just as well talk to myself.'

Fanny Clarke averted her eyes from the fine cobweb that hung from the plastic reproduction chandelier. 'I know exactly how you feel, Mrs Norkette. Knobby is just the same. Want anything doing around the house and you might as well ask for a rocket trip to the moon. Unless, of course, it affects his food, drink or his sex.'

Mrs Norkette couldn't believe her ears. She raised an enquiring eyebrow. 'He's not still bothering you, surely? Not at your time of life.'

'Bothering me?' giggled Fanny, inspecting the Wedgwood jug on the sideboard. 'I wouldn't put it quite like that. It's just that he doesn't leave me alone. Ever since he was made redundant he wants it all the time – and not just the missionary position, I can tell you. He says he's only making up for lost opportunities when he was fully employed on the night shift at the sack and jute factory.'

Mrs Norkette sniffed disdainfully and discreetly pulled away from her new-found friend.

'Well, thank goodness I can't say the same for my Frank in that department. He's in a funny mood of late; perhaps it's the male menopause. He shows more interest in polishing his woods, or beating himself at cribbage.'

Fanny Clarke slurped loudly from her cup and shook her head in sympathy. 'My Knobby has some funny turns as well. He got up in the middle of the night last week – I think it was Wednesday, or maybe it was Thursday, I can't remember which ... anyway it doesn't matter. Well, as I say, he got up in the middle of the night to relieve himself – I mean visit the bathroom of course, not the other sort – and when he got back into bed he was wearing one of my shortie night-dresses. Well, I ask you! When I enquired what he was playing at he said he must have put it on by mistake in the dark. Which reminds me, I'm missing a pair of my red flannelette drawers which I wear in bed when it's cold. Not that I have them on very long these days. Do you think I've got sufficient grounds to write up to one of them Agony Aunts? Maureen Loudmouth in the Evening Post is supposed to be very good.'

Mrs Norkette had no inclination of being drawn into mundane banter with a woman who had a mouth like a machine gun. She thought Knobby probably demanded copious amounts of sex just to give her mouth a rest. She rose impatiently and looked out of the kitchen window.

'What are those two doing out there? Their teas have gone stone cold.'

Fanny ran her long scarlet fingernails along the intricate beading which framed the wall mirror, then she flicked her fingers across the books in the bookcase. 'I think my better half is helping Frank to repair the saddle on his bike. Your Frank had us in stitches in the car. He complained he'd been suffering nightmares of late with his piles. Every time he rode over a bump it was like having a red hot poker thrust between his buttocks.'

Mrs Norkette again sighed inwardly. Her husband didn't need to discus his medical ailments with complete strangers; he could be very crude at times. She also wished Fanny would stop fingering her things. Now she busied herself smelling the flowers and examining the underside of the Greek urn. Where did she think she was, at a car boot sale?

'Do you still work, Mrs Norkette? Or, as they say, are you comfortably retired?'

'I took early retirement,' Mrs Norkette replied, looking Fanny straight in the eyes as if to say, 'and I'm not telling you exactly how early.' Comfortable is another matter, but I do a couple of afternoons in the charity shops – one for the children and one for the animals. And you? She wasn't really interested but she thought she had better ask.

'I work three days a week in the Invalid Bath and Toilet Centre in Crown Street. It's a job share. I share it with a

black gentleman who lives with his invalid wife in the
sheltered bungalows in Jepthune Court.'

'And what is it you share?' asked Mrs Norkette, wanting
to take the cups and saucers back into the kitchen but
fearing to leave Fanny to her own devices.

'We demonstrate the invalid baths and toilets. Mr Belcher,
the owner, says I'm getting quite professional at it. If ever
you're in need of one I could get you a nice bit of discount.
The invalid toilets with adjustable seats and pneumatic
water sprayer are selling really well at the moment.'

'Yes, well I should imagine they are,' replied Mrs Norkette,
hardly bearing to imagine them at all. 'But surely you're
not expected to demonstrate the baths to each and every
customer who comes into the shop?'

'Of course. Me and my black gentleman friend, that's
our job.'

'But you'll catch your death of cold and your skin will
finish up all wrinkly, in and out of those baths all the
time.'

Fanny Clarke's chest heaved and she erupted into laughter
with a high pitched staccato cackle that put Mrs Norkette's
teeth on edge.

'Don't be silly. I only do a dry run. Who do you think I am, Lady Godiva? My skin is wrinkly enough without giving it a good soaking every half an hour.'

Mrs Norkette felt relieved when the back door opened and the two husbands ambled into the kitchen.

'This is she, the one who must be obeyed,' introduced Frank. 'And this fine figure of a man is Knobby, husband of Fanny. Hilarious isn't it? Fanny and Knobby – sounds like a music hall double act.'

Mrs Norkette accepted the outstretched hand; it felt warm and damp. She took in Knobby's rotund figure and his equally rounded face, topped off with a completely bald head with a few tufts of hair poking out defiantly from behind both ears. With his thick, oval-rimmed glasses he resembled an ageing Billy Bunter.

Frank patted his friend on the back. 'Thanks to Knobby we've sorted out my rear end. It was a bit raggedy and worn, but I think we've made quite a respectable job of it. Parking my posterior on that saddle will be like sitting on a bale of feathers.'

Mrs Norkette watched carefully as the two men moved out of the kitchen and into the lounge/diner.

'I hope your feet are clean. I've just hoovered that carpet.'

'My feet are perfectly clean. It's my boots that might be a bit mucky,' retorted Frank.

'Is that supposed to be funny?' asked Mrs Norkette with a face like a wet weekend.

'Well, it was an attempt,' said Frank, digging Knobby in the ribs. 'I know it wasn't "funny hilarious" or anything like that, just an attempt to get the evening off with a light hearted swing.'

'You'll swing all right if you make a mess on the carpet. If you want a fresh cup of tea you can make your own. I haven't got time to keep getting up and down just to make cups of tea for you to leave getting cold.'

Frank ignored the offer of tea and opened the drinks cabinet. 'Lighten up, woman, will you. I thought I had invited my friends round for an evening of fun and frivolity. I'm sure they don't want to hear your mouth going full throttle, nagging me into a state of utter exhaustion. What do you fancy, Knobby? Shall we crack open a bottle to launch my refurbished saddle? God bless her and all lucky enough to get their leg over. How about a nice whiskey and soda?'

'Whiskey and ginger would be preferable,' replied Knobby wringing his hands in anticipation.

'I suppose it would, if we had any ginger. This isn't the function room of the Grand hotel. You'll have to make do with soda.'

'In that case, I'll settle for water,' conceded a disappointed Knobby.

'You can be right awkward at times, Knobby Clark – just like on the bowling green. I've seen you pull a face because I've told you to come in on your forehand instead of your backhand. And now you're doing it again because there's no carbonated ginger. Water you say? Well, here's a pint glass; the tap is in the kitchen. You avail yourself of as much Adam's ale as you can drink.'

Knobby's face paled. 'I meant a drop of water with my whiskey,' he stammered.

'He knows very well what you mean, Knobby. He's just being cantankerous. As I've explained Fanny, he's been in a right funny mood of late,' scolded Mrs Norkette.

'I wished you'd make up your mind, woman,' protested Frank. 'When I tried to be funny you said I wasn't, and when I don't say anything funny you accuse me of acting funny.'

'Frank Norkette, you can be right exasperating at times.'

'Now steady on, woman. You've not swallowed our leather bound Concise Oxford dictionary have you? Cantankerous?

Exasperating? If we're playing spelling bees tonight you Clarkes have got no chance. Now come on, ladies, enough of this jocular banter. What are you having to drink?'

'How about a nice sherry?' Mrs Norkette asked of her lady guest. 'We're fortunate to have several to choose from.'

'Sounds lovely to me,' accepted Fanny, relieved that the verbal sparring between her hosts appeared to be abating. Frank spun the revolving drinks tray around at an alarming rate. The bottles wobbled and the glasses clinked.

'Now what would you call a nice sherry? Would that be a light sherry? Or a dark sherry? Or perhaps a traditional cream sherry? Or even this little bottle of cooking sherry that appears to have evaporated rather rapidly over the last few days.'

'Just pour out two cream sherries and then sit yourself down at the table.' Mrs Norkette's face had taken on the appearance of a badly nicotine stained net curtain. Frank's countenance bore a deliberate look of defiance as he fiddled with his hi-fi system. 'I'll just put a couple of records on. I can't abide long lingering silences.'

Mrs Norkette eyed his every move. 'We'll want to hear ourselves think.'

'I'm not sure if I've got that particular tune in my record collection, petal. "Ourselves Think". Who sings it? Not The Moonbeams, is it? Or Anne Shelton?'

Mrs Norkette's upper lip drew back visibly as she pulled out a chair for Fanny. 'See. There's just no talking to him. I mean we don't want it too loud.'

Frank pressed the start button with a flourish. 'It's only for a little background music. No need to get your passion killers in a twist.' Anne Ziegler and Webster Booth commenced their gentle harmonising of 'We'll gather lilacs'.

Knobby Clarke placed the boxed game of Trivial Pursuit in the middle of the table. His beady eyes scanned his audience with gleeful anticipation.

'What's this little box of tricks you've got here then?' asked Frank, downing his drink in one and licking his lips.

'It's called Trivial Pursuit.'

'I thought it might be,' commented Frank tersely, 'being as it has got "Trivial Pursuit" plastered all over it.'

'It's a simple game of general knowledge.'

Frank inspected the box from end to end and the lid from side to side, as if it concealed some sort of booby trap. 'When you say that,' he enquired, 'do you mean it's simply a game, or a simple game? There is a marked difference between the two.'

'I've warned you,' threatened Mrs Norkette, waving a firm finger at her errant husband. She smiled sweetly at her guests. 'Another drink everyone? I think we're going to need it.'

With great deliberation Knobby spread open the multicoloured board. He pushed a box containing half the questions to Frank and kept a box containing the rest of the questions for himself. Frank immediately swapped the boxes over.

'What have you done that for?' asked Mrs Norkette, struggling to snatch the box from Frank's grasp.

'How do we know they haven't doctored the questions before they got here? Kept the easy ones for themselves and given us the hard ones. We'd look a right pair of prunes then, wouldn't we?'

'My goodness!' exclaimed Fanny, shaking her head in disbelief. 'Do you really think we would stoop so low? Give him both boxes, dearest. Let him make his own choice.'

Frank, perhaps fearing a double bluff, held onto the box he already had. Knobby breathed a sigh of relief.

'Right. Everybody happy? The idea of the game is that each team moves a plastic container around the board in conjunction with a throw of the dice. When you answer a specific question you receive a plastic chip to put into each segment. The first team to fill up all the segments is declared the winner. It's as simple as that.'

Frank picked up his container and after turning it over several times swapped it for a different one. 'Would you mind repeating that?'

Knobby frowned back. 'Do I have to? It's dead simple; an idiot can play it.'

Frank gave his wife a playful elbow. 'Right, petal, get your thinking cap on. You should be champion at this.'

Mrs Norkette spluttered into her sherry and, before she could retaliate, Knobby took the opportunity to roll the dice. He moved his container four places across the board.

'What do you think you're doing?' challenged Frank, flicking though the rule book.

'What does it look like? I'm starting the game. I've thrown a four, so we move four places.'

Frank clicked his tongue around his teeth and shook his head. He picked up the marker and placed it back to the centre of the board. 'Not so fast, pal. According to this book, rule number one. "The game shall commence by the team rolling the highest score".' He pushed the dice across to Mrs Norkette. 'You do the honours, petal. Roll the dice and try to beat a four.'

Knobby glared silently back at his opponent while Mrs Norkette pushed her chair back, blew hard on the dice and threw it across the table. The dice glanced off the two glasses of sherry, rebounded against the bowl filled with salted peanuts and ricocheted off the table onto the sheepskin rug in front of the fireplace. Frank slipped out of his chair and retrieved the dice.

'It's a six!'

'You can't have that,' snapped Fanny.

'And why not?'

'It's obvious, isn't it? You'll be throwing the dice all

round the room, getting up first and claiming it's a six every time.'

'Quite right, Fanny,' said Knobby, giving his wife a knowing smile. 'I think it only fair that the dice must finish on the table where everybody can see it.'

Frank grinned across at Knobby. 'This game's not as simple as we first thought then.'

He threw the dice but could only manage a three. Knobby commandeered the dice and kicked off with a five. He made a great show of counting out the squares.

'That will be the Entertainment category. You have to pick the first card out of the box and ask the question indicated by the pink square.'

Mrs Norkette fumbled out a card and held it secretly against her bosom. She glanced at it briefly. 'Ringo Starr.'

There followed a brief silence.

'Ringo Starr? What sort of question is that?' asked Knobby, draining his whiskey and helping himself to some salted peanuts.

'How do we know? It's *your* flipping game,' chortled Frank.

Fanny leaned over and tried to look at the card. Mrs Norkette turned away and clasped it even closer to her bosom.

'That's right, girl. Don't let them have a free look,' encouraged Frank, thumbing rapidly through the rule book. 'It doesn't say anything in here about opponents having a sly look before giving their answer.'

Fanny covered her eyes with both hands and shook her head in disbelief. 'I wasn't trying to cheat, if that's what you are insinuating, but if Mrs Norkette turns the card over she might find she has mistakenly read out the answer instead of the question.'

Mrs Norkette turned the card over. 'Who was the oldest member of the Beatles? Oh dear, have I done it wrong then?'

Frank laughed into his whiskey. 'You said it, petal. Upside down and back to front. You were spot on, Knobby, when you said it was a simple game. They don't come any simpler than my missus.'

Mrs Norkette threw the card down on the table.

'Temper, temper,' said Frank. 'Keep your wig on, woman, it's only a game. Who's ready for another drink? I know I am – the excitement is all getting a bit too much for me.'

Knobby sipped gratefully at his fresh drink. 'Shall we continue?' Anyone can make a mistake. Just pick another card and make sure you read out the question instead of the answer.'

Mrs Norkette extracted a second card from the box and scrutinised it carefully. 'Who was the cook in "Upstairs, Downstairs"?'

'Mrs Bridges!' answered Knobby quickly. For his pains he received an elbow in the ribs from Fanny.

'We're supposed to be a team. We should confer before giving an answer.'

'Well, who do *you* think it is?'

'Mrs Bridges. I was just about to tell you.'

'Right then. We both agree it's Mrs Bridges.'

'Stroll on,' murmured Frank. 'If we carry on at this rate we'll be here all night.'

'Is that your final answer?' asked Mrs Norkette.

'Yes, Mrs Bridges.'

'Well, you're both wrong. It's Cliff Richard.'

Another interval of silence followed.

'What are you talking about, woman? It can't be Cliff Richard,' moaned Knobby.

'Well, that's what it says in black and white,' retorted Mrs Norkette.

'Let me have a look,' said Fanny, almost snatching the card away. A second card fell to the floor.

209

'Oh dear, silly me! There were two cards stuck together.' Knobby rubbed his eyes in bewilderment and turned the second card over. 'There you are – Mrs Bridges. I knew I was right all along.'

'All right, clever clogs,' interrupted Frank. 'You'll just have to make allowances for my wife. I did warn you she was a bit on the simple side.'

Mrs Norkette pushed her chair away and stormed into the kitchen. 'I'm warning you. You'll push me too far and then you'll be sorry.' She returned with a forced smile on her face and placed a tray of sausage rolls at one end of the table and a tray of buttered crumpets at the other. Plates and napkins were manoeuvred into the centre.

'You're very kind,' said Knobby forgivingly as he handed round the plates. They munched contentedly for a while and then continued the game. Fanny wiped her fingers with a napkin and rolled the dice. The marker landed on a green square.

'That's Science and Nature, isn't it? I'm not very good at those subjects.'

'Don't worry, my love. I'm right by your side,' encouraged Knobby. Mrs Norkette read out the question slowly.

'Where is the human skin least sensitive?'

Knobby and Fanny looked vaguely at each other.

'Dead easy! A giveaway!' exclaimed Frank.

'It is?' asked Knobby.

'Of course, everybody knows the skin's least sensitive area is around my wife's brainbox.'

Mrs Norkette slammed the box of cards down in disgust. The plastic marker slid across the board and half the peanuts joined in the game. 'You're getting right up my gander, Frank Norkette. I've had just about as much as I can stand.'

'Here, goosey, goosey...' tormented Frank.

Mrs Norkette lunged clumsily at her husband with a

210

clenched fist, but Frank, well used to her sudden uprisings spotted it coming and swayed deftly out of harm's way. Knobby was not so quick and the blow caught him on the side of the head, knocking his glasses flying. Momentarily stunned he slumped forward, inadvertently tipping the board. Dice and markers bounced into the air. Frank slid off his chair in fits of laughter. The two women rushed to Knobby's aid.

'I'm right sorry, Fanny. That was meant for Frank, not for you, Knobby. Are you all right, Mr Clarke? Are you all right?'

Knobby blinked, shook his head in disbelief at what had happened and then replaced his glasses. 'I think so,' he muttered, 'My, that's some wallop you pack there, Mrs Norkette. I wouldn't like to be on the receiving end of one of them every day.' He set his empty glass upright. 'Do you think I could have a refill? Just for medicinal purposes.'

'Of course you can. I'm really sorry. You know I didn't mean it.' Mrs Norkette inspected the side of Knobby's head. 'You've got a nasty welt coming up there; you'd better have a double.'

Frank recovered quickly from his laughing fit. 'That's my best whiskey you're talking about. Don't go spraying it about like water.'

The next record dropped onto the turntable. Perry Como sang 'Magic Moments'. After surveying Knobby's injuries and giving him the all clear, Frank ruffled what remained of Knobby's hair.

'What does she get for that little show of petulance? Must be a red card surely. That's a sending off offence, striking an opponent, Send her off for an early bath and fine her for unlady-like conduct.'

'You know full well that was meant for you,' complained Mrs Norkette. 'You're not supposed to move out of the way when I'm going to hit you.'

Fanny straightened the board and replaced the markers. 'Shall we continue?' she asked, a little warily. 'It's your turn to throw the dice.'

Mrs Norkette took care to throw the dice a little more gently this time, and Frank counted out the necessary squares. Fanny pulled the question out of the box. She put her hand over her mouth and started giggling.

'Where does a Vietnamese deposit his Dong?'

Mrs Norkette gasped.

'You're making it up,' declared Frank.

'I'm not,' protested Fanny. To prove it she slid the card to her husband.

'Perfectly straightforward. Where does a Vietnamese deposit his Dong?'

'Stupid question, if you ask me.' Frank turned to his wife. 'Come on petal, you're quite well up in the anatomy department. Where would he put his perishing Dong?'

'I wouldn't like to say. It doesn't sound very pleasant to me.'

'Do you give up?' asked Fanny impatiently. Frank inspected the soles of his shoes, then picked at the fluff in his trouser turnups. Mrs Norkette gazed up at the ceiling as if expecting some shaft of divine inspiration to issue from the plastic chandelier.

'Time's up,' declared Knobby, consulting his watch.

'He deposits it in the bank!' exclaimed Fanny and Knobby in unison.

'Well, he would do, wouldn't he?' grumbled Frank. 'Stupid question. Are there any more gems in the box like that? Because if there are I'm retiring to the bathroom to clip my toenails and pummystone my bunions. It will be a damn sight more interesting.'

Knobby threw the dice again and Mrs Norkette took great care to select only a single card.

'What event was Moses most famous for?'

'The receiving of the ten commandments,' answered Knobby almost instantly.

'Knobby!' scolded Fanny.

'Oh sorry, dearest, I forgot. What do *you* think?'

'I haven't the faintest. I'll go along with you.'

Knobby stroked the top of his wife's hand. I must admit I am quite well versed in the bible, which rather leaves others at a disadvantage.'

'It doesn't matter, you're both wrong,' declared Mrs Norkette. 'The answer on my card is "The four hundred metres hurdles".'

Once more a brief silence ensued. Knobby snatched the card from Mrs Norkette's grasp.

'You silly woman! It's Ed Moses!'

'I'm sorry. I thought they were his initials,' whimpered Mrs Norkette.

'And just who do you think you're calling silly? That's my wife you're talking about,' threatened Frank.

'Well, how can we play the game? She can't even read out a simple question or answer. She hasn't got one right yet.'

'You're the one who said it was a game for simpletons, and my wife happens to be an expert in that department, but it doesn't give you the right to cast aspersions on her senility. You've got a nerve. You come round here, eat our food, drink our drink and then turn on the hands that feed you!'

'I'm not turning,' protested Knobby, his face paling under the accusations.

'You are, pal!' shouted Frank squaring up. 'You're turning round and clearing off to where you came from.'

Fanny scooped up the game and grabbed hold of her husband's arm. 'Come on, Knobby, it's time we left.' She turned to Mrs Norkette. 'I would like to thank you for a lovely evening, but it's a shame your husband can't hold his drink or his temper and behave in a more civilised manner.' They scurried from the house without any goodbyes.

Mrs Norkette sank into an armchair, her head in her hands. 'A complete disaster, a complete and utter disaster. I'll be pointed out and vilified when I go to the bingo. I won't be able to show my face at the annual dinner and dance.'

'Well, don't go blaming me,' said Frank. 'I was only standing up for you, as any loyal husband would. They were a funny couple anyway. I'll tell you what, petal, all this shouting and excitement has made me ravenous. Are there any more buttered crumpets?'

The final record dropped onto the turntable. Billy Cotton and his band praised the delights of 'Friends and Neighbours'.

12

Sweet Smell of Revenge

'The question is, Mrs Boot, did you or did you not shout out at a crucial point in the game: "My husband's balls are bigger than your husband's"?'

At this delicate stage of the proceedings, the thin lower lip of Maud Wilcox, President of Clopthorne Ladies' Bowls Club, visibly trembled with distaste. She felt it below her dignity to have to deal with this measure of coarseness.

On the other hand, Amy Boot took things in her stride. She wrinkled her nose up and down, tilted her head slightly and finger-combed at the greying curls behind her right ear. Finally, she readjusted her spectacles.

'Of course I did. You must have about a dozen witnesses who heard me say it.'

The club president placed her notes on the table in front of her with a flourish of triumph.

'In that case, you do not refute the charges of bringing the game and, more importantly, the club, into disrepute?'

'Of course I do,' protested Amy. 'It was just a slip of the tongue. All right, I should have said "bowls" or "woods". I just got carried away in the heat of the moment. There is absolutely no need for this stupid witch hunt.'

Maud Wilcox retrieved her notes, her badge of office swinging loosely from its mauve and yellow ribbon. Her sense of well-being this afternoon was tempered by the previous evening's disastrous application of a new colour wash to her hair. Bright henna was not the effect she had desired. She pulled her hat down further to hide the embarrassment.

'Mr and Mrs Lovitt further complain that both you and your husband used derogatory language throughout the match in an attempt to put them off their game – in fact, right up to the time the unfortunate Mr Lovitt was rushed off to hospital.'

Amy Boot threw back her ample shoulders and interrupted.

'All I said was that Mr Lovitt was playing like a giraffe.'

'And what exactly did you mean by that?'

'His balls – sorry – his woods were a long way from his head. It's quite a well known saying in the game. Surely you must have heard it before?'

'I can't say that I have, Mrs Boot.'

'Then you are very fortunate to have led such a sheltered life,' retorted Amy witheringly.

A flush of annoyance suffused the unsmiling face of Maud Wilcox. She was not used to having her authority usurped.

'That's as maybe, but I am not the one under examination here. Now the accident to Mr Lovitt. Would you like to give your side of the story?'

The other lady members of the committee either nodded knowingly to each other or shook their heads in disapproval. Their immaculate turn-out in full bowling attire, hats positioned squarely on newly permed heads and badges of minor office catching the dying rays of the afternoon sun, gave the appearance of a military tribunal. The normally pleasant and bubbly atmosphere of the clubhouse had taken on the hushed solemnity of a courtroom.

Amy Boot slowly folded her plump arms across her ample bosom, forcing her club cravat to stick out like a defiant tongue.

'As I remember it, on the end in question, I had one

wood left and we were five shots down. The strategy was simple. I would have to go for an all out drive. It was unfortunate that Mr Lovitt failed to pull his foot out of the way in time.' Amy shrugged her shoulders. 'As far as I am concerned, it was a complete accident.'

'An accident indeed!' roared Maud Wilcox straining out of her chair. 'After fracturing Mr Lovitt's ankle in three places, there was still enough venomous power in the wood for it to bounce it off the edge of the green, through the wicker fence and across the lake like a Barnes-Wallace bomb where it decapitated a rare and expensive ornamental duck. It was a case of unnecessary force endangering life and property for which the club has been forced to make costly recompense.'

A thin film of perspiration began to penetrate the fragile barriers of Maud Wilcox's make up.

Amy Boot remained placid.

'I admit it was very unfortunate, but at least one good thing came out of it.'

'Good thing? And pray what might that have been?'

'It killed the end,' announced Amy proudly.

'Killed the end, indeed. It very nearly killed everything in its wake.' The Club President turned to her committee for assurance. They backed her authority and wisdom with suitable murmurings and shaking of heads.

'To continue, Mrs Boot...'

'Amy, for crying out loud. You all know my name is Amy.'

'That's all very well, Mrs Boot, but as these charges are of a serious nature, we prefer to keep proceedings formal.'

Outside, the late afternoon sunshine fought a losing battle against sombre clouds. Intermittent raindrops splashed the clubhouse windows. The flower heads on the floribunda roses swayed gently in the freshening breeze. A discarded plastic bag cart-wheeled erratically across the deserted green. Inside, the President continued her inquisition.

'The third charge on our list, unfortunately no lesser than the other two, pertains to your intolerable behaviour in the annual match against the Repentant Ladies of Saint Mary's Corrective Institution. Your shouting, screaming and eventual walking out threw the whole game into complete chaos. No wonder the visitors scrambled back onto their coach and returned swiftly and without ceremony to the safety of their prison walls.'

Maud paused briefly to recover her breath and composure. 'What have you got to say to this charge?'

Amy Boot uncrossed her stout legs and brushed down the pleats of her grey skirt. A mischievous smile flickered across her face.

'Believe you me, I've got plenty to say, and this is the first chance I've had to say it. I should warn you that any of the committee who suffer from bad nerves and weak constitutions should leave the room immediately. That includes you, Mrs Trumpington.'

Sybil Trumpington, a thin, fragile individual visibly blanched and backed away. She fingered her captain's badge nervously.

Maud Wilcox rose to her feet and waved her finger.

'I warn you, Mrs Boot. I will not stand for any character assassinations in this room. Any personal abuse and you will be thrown out of the club!'

218

Amy jumped to her feet and eyeballed the President.
'By you and who else?'
'I was speaking figuratively of course,' replied Maud
Wilcox cautiously. 'Now say your piece and keep it civil.'
Amy ceased cracking her knuckles, much to the relief
of Mrs Trumpington.

'Mrs President, how would you have liked to skip the
rink the Club Captain presented me with, in her infinite
wisdom, last Saturday? While I must point out that I have
absolutely nothing against the three ladies personally, the
combination of those three personalities would have tested
the patience of Mother Teresa herself, God rest her soul.
I might just as well have stayed at home and soaked my
bunions.

To begin with, who in their right mind, would put Brenda
Braithwaite down as a lead? The poor woman has only
got one eye and the other is about as much use as a candle
in a hurricane. She couldn't find the jack, she couldn't
find her own woods and she kept wandering off so we
couldn't find her. When we *did* find her, she couldn't keep
the jack on the rink, never mind her woods. Every time I
reminded her which rink we were supposed to be playing
on she took it so personally she nearly suffered a nervous
breakdown. Her wailing and sobbing upset all the youngsters
in the children's play area on the other side of the putting
green. It was like a madhouse!'

Amy paused momentarily, took a deep breath, then
ploughed on with her explanations like a politician on speed.

'As if that wasn't bad enough, who did I have as a
number two? Gertrude McFadgin. Her credentials are, I
admit, beyond reproach – Captain of Lancashire Ladies
sixty-five times, selected to play for England on twenty-
three occasions, has won every competition the game has
to offer. Undoubtedly, the best player this club has ever
produced. But that was sixty years ago. The woman is now

219

a hundred and one! Every one of her woods finished up nearer her than me. I had to ask her how she was doing. Then she kept forgetting her score card. She would totter back every end to retrieve it. By the time we had finished the first end every other rink had completed five or six. We would still have been out there at midnight.

To cap it all, I was given honorary life member, Elsie Clackworthy, as my number three. We all know Elsie is a whizzkid on the social side of the club. Want anything organised, send for Elsie: raffles, tombola, social dances. Her sausage rolls and home made ginger beer are alone worth turning up at matches for. Her Victoria sponges knock spots off all the television cooks'. But her bowling skills come nowhere near her social attributes. Plus, one must not forget, she possesses an added bonus every skip could wish for. She's as deaf as a post! I'm very sorry for her, but her erratic sign language made her look like a bookie's tic-tac man having an epileptic fit. I couldn't tell if we were holding ten shots or down by a handful.'

Mrs Trumpington finally summoned up enough courage to throw in her two penny worth.

'That was no excuse to throw the scoreboard into the lake and hurl woods in all directions.'

Amy responded like a viper bitten. She jumped to her feet and waved a podgy fist in front of the captain's face. Mrs Trumpington's tortoiseshell-rimmed spectacles slid to the very end of her pointed nose.

'It's all right for you, Mrs Bloody Captain. The three players in front of you were all county players. Talk about a loaded rink. It must have been very pleasant and rewarding for you, standing there turning your score over by the handful.'

Mrs Trumpington rose tentatively to her feet. 'Well, I've never been so insulted in all my life.'

'I bet you haven't!' challenged Amy, cracking her knuckles and daring the captain to make any sort of move which could be construed as the slightest hint of a threat.

'I would have liked to see you trying to cope with the female version of The Crazy Gang. I know I'm not the most popular person in this club, but I had the funny feeling of having been deliberately set up. I half expected Jeremy Beadle and his candid camera crew to walk onto the green.'

Surprisingly, under the circumstances, Amy Boot evaded a ban, a fine, or even the ignominy of being thrown out of Clopthorne Ladies' Bowls Club. She never allowed them the satisfaction of passing judgement. Instead, she resigned.

Two days later, she returned with a holdall and vacated her locker. On her way out she slammed the door so violently all the windows rattled and the portrait of the club founder – Mrs Imogen Thomas, Hon. Life Member – jumped off its hook and crashed to the floor amid a shower of broken glass. Amy's final act of defiance was to throw her locker key into the boating lake.

It could be said that Amy Boot, during her two year membership of the club, had caused a bit of a stink. But that was nothing compared to the smell for which she was responsible weeks after her departure – an obnoxious, sneaking odour that gradually spread its tentacles throughout every nook and cranny of the clubhouse.

At first, a body hunt was organised in case Gertrude McFadgin, at her great age, had decided to crawl away into some corner, like a condemned dog, to die. Eventually, she was located, alive and well, furtively treating her ancient woods against woodworm. The smell grew stronger by the day. Towards the weekend, with the sun high in a clear blue sky, one needed a large perfumed handkerchief over the face to enter the clubhouse. The friendly fixture, scheduled against the Lancashire Past Presidents' Touring Team, had to be cancelled.

The following Monday, hedgehogs, mice, spiders and other assorted creatures vacated their temporary homes in disgust. The man from Dyno-Rod was summoned to flush out the toilets and drainage system, but the strengthening smell continued to pervade every corner. The crimson and cream flock wallpaper in the dining area, so often in the past a topic of conversation at tea breaks, began to curl up at the edges. In the toilets, the tiles began sliding down the walls.

By Friday, giant bluebottles were spotted endeavouring to escape from Amy Boot's abandoned locker. The spare key couldn't be located and the locksmith was called in. When he finally broke in it needed four of the stoutest lady members to carry him out into the fresh air and in turn eagerly apply mouth to mouth resuscitation.

Inside the locker, on the shelf usually reserved for shoes and bags, the rotting remains of a large cod heaved and throbbed with a mass wriggling of maggots. A piece of cardboard pinned through the centre of an unblinking eye bore a short but meaningful message: 'UP YOURS'.

It took a further two weeks to rid the clubhouse of the smell. Teams of volunteers worked furiously in relays, scrubbing and fumigating. Half a dozen automatic 'fresh air' dispensers were placed at strategic points around the building. Filling the gaps, generous bunches of lavender, lily of the valley and sweetpeas helped revitalise the atmosphere. Gradually, the putrid stench drifted away. Woodlice, ants and spiders returned to rebuild homes in the dark recesses of the clubhouse and the gentle click-clacking of colliding bowls could once more be heard echoing around the peaceful greens.